SNOT CHOCOLATE

Morris Gleitzman grew up in England and went to live in Australia when he was sixteen. He worked as a frozen-chicken thawer, sugar-mill rolling-stock unhooker, fashion-industry trainee, department-store Santa, TV producer, newspaper columnist and screenwriter. Then he had a wonderful experience. He wrote a novel for young people. Now he's one of the bestselling children's authors in Australia. He lives in Brisbane and Sydney and visits Britain regularly. His many books include *Two Weeks with the Queen*, *Bumface*, *Boy Overboard* and *Once*.

Visit Morris at his website:
morrisgleitzman.com

Also by Morris Gleitzman

Adults Only
Aristotle's Nostril
Belly Flop
Blabber Mouth
Boy Overboard
Bumface
Deadly! (with Paul Jennings)
Doubting Thomas
Gift of the Gab
Girl Underground
Give Peas a Chance
Grace
Misery Guts
The Other Facts of Life
Pizza Cake
Puppy Fat
Second Childhood
Sticky Beak
Teacher's Pet
Toad Away
Toad Heaven
Toad Rage
Toad Surprise
Toad Delight
Too Small to Fail
Wicked! (with Paul Jennings)
Two Weeks with the Queen
Worm Story
Worry Warts
Once
Then
Now
After
Soon

SNOT CHOCOLATE

MORRIS GLEITZMAN

PUFFIN

PUFFIN BOOKS

UK | USA | Canada | Ireland | Australia
India | New Zealand | South Africa

Puffin Books is part of the Penguin Random House group of companies
whose addresses can be found at global.penguinrandomhouse.com.

www.penguin.co.uk
www.puffin.co.uk
www.ladybird.co.uk

First published by Penguin Random House Australia 2016
Published in Great Britain by Puffin Books 2017

001

Internal design by Tony Palmer
Typeset in 13/15pt Minion Regular
Printed in Great Britain by Clays Ltd, St Ives plc

A CIP catalogue record for this book is available from the British Library

ISBN: 978–0–141–37525–0

All correspondence to:
Puffin Books,
Penguin Random House Children's,
80 Strand, London WC2R 0RL

For Gracie

Contents

King Ned

Ned opened his eyes and frowned.

Something was wrong.

It was daylight and he was still in bed.

How was that possible? Uncle Vern didn't allow sleeping in. The hovel was too small. Uncle Vern and Ned always got up at dawn in case the pigs needed a lie-down.

Something else doesn't feel right, thought Ned.

I'm warm.

Deliciously warm.

Ned saw why. A blanket was draped over him. Uncle Vern's blanket. Ned recognised the sheepskin with the sheep's head still attached.

Which was very strange, because Uncle Vern didn't believe in young people being warm.

'Not good for ye,' Uncle Vern often told Ned. 'That be what caused the terrible infant mortality in the twelfth century, children bein' too warm.

1

Either that or too hungry, I can't remember zackly.'

Ned didn't care if being snug was dangerous.

He was enjoying it.

Anyway, he thought, this isn't the twelfth century, it's the thirteenth, so I'll probably survive.

Ned had never felt warm in bed before. It was lovely. He snuggled deeper under the blanket. The bed felt extra soft, as if somebody had stuffed extra straw and rags and fluffy dead mice into the mattress while he slept.

'Good mornin', sire.'

Ned jumped guiltily.

He'd assumed Uncle Vern had gone out to get some stoats for breakfast. But this was definitely Uncle Vern's voice.

Ned peered around. The hovel wasn't much bigger than a plague cart so it was strange that he could hear Uncle Vern but not see him.

Puzzled, Ned sat up.

And stared in surprise.

Uncle Vern was splayed out on the ground next to the bed, bottom in the air, chin in the dirt, staring up at him fearfully.

'I await your command, sire,' said Uncle Vern.

If Uncle Vern had been a different sort of person, given to light-hearted japes rather than scraping mould off damp trees for a living, Ned might have thought this was a merry jest.

But Uncle Vern didn't do merry jests.

What was going on?

'Uncle Vern,' said Ned, concerned. 'You shouldn't lie on the damp ground like that. You'll get skin rot.'

'No I won't,' said Uncle Vern, still looking at Ned fearfully.

'Millipedes might crawl up your nose,' said Ned, desperately trying to think of something to snap Uncle Vern out of it.

Uncle Vern shook his head. Ned wasn't sure if he was disagreeing or trying to dislodge millipedes that had already crawled in.

'Why are you doing this?' said Ned.

Uncle Vern was a stern and rather bossy uncle who spent a lot of time calling Ned a fool. Sprawling on the ground and twitching in terror just wasn't like him.

'I'm doin' this so as you won't be killin' me,' stammered Uncle Vern. 'Your Highness.'

Ned stared at him, very concerned.

Your Highness?

Poor Uncle Vern must have accidentally swallowed some tree mould while he was feeding it to the pigs and it must have given him a tragic affliction of the brain.

Slowly, so as not to scare Uncle Vern, Ned climbed out of bed.

Uncle Vern slithered further away.

'Uncle Vern,' said Ned gently. 'You only call people Your Highness when they're the king. I'm not the king.'

'Yes you are,' said Uncle Vern.

Ned wondered what to do.

They couldn't afford a doctor, and he wasn't sure if acorn tea could cure a brain affliction this bad. Perhaps if he used some of the really strong acorns, the ones that had been eaten by pigs and come out the other end . . .

He bent down to help Uncle Vern up.

Uncle Vern whimpered and tried to slither even further away. Which wasn't easy in a tiny hovel cluttered up with two beds and two stools.

Ned decided to humour Uncle Vern. He couldn't think what else to do.

'Sit yourself on a stool,' he said nervously. 'That's a command.'

Ned suspected that commands weren't usually issued in a wobbly voice, but Uncle Vern didn't seem to notice. He scrambled to his feet. Then hesitated. Ned guessed he must be terrified about sitting down when royalty was still standing.

Ned gave a regal nod.

Uncle Vern sat on a stool, still looking terrified.

'Don't be afraid,' said Ned. 'I'm not going to hurt you. Kings don't kill people.'

'Yes they do,' said Uncle Vern. 'The last king, God rest his soul, used to kill people all the time. That's why he was called King Rufus The People Killer.'

Ned hadn't known that. Plus it sounded like the king was dead, which he hadn't known either. Even after living with Uncle Vern for two years, Ned was still getting used to how much time news took to reach people living in remote bogs with pigs who had bowel problems.

Except, Ned reminded himself, Uncle Vern isn't thinking straight, so probably none of this is true. The king probably isn't dead at all. He's probably in his castle right now, handing out wise advice and food parcels to his subjects.

'The king didn't have any sons,' said Uncle Vern. 'So they've been looking for the next in line to the throne. They came round here in the middle of the night while you were asleep and said it was you.'

Ned sighed sadly.

Uncle Vern was in the grip of a terrible malady.

A sudden one. Like when Mum and Dad got the plague. One minute they were perfectly healthy, the next you were at their funeral.

Ned didn't want to think about that.

He also didn't want to think about what lay ahead for Uncle Vern if he couldn't be cured. Times were tough these days for brain-addled lunatics. They usually got drowned in duckponds, or locked in a cage and exhibited at fairs, or sometimes both.

Ned patted Uncle Vern on the arm and while Uncle Vern hid under a stool, he hurried out of the hovel desperately hoping there were some strong acorns in the pig pen.

Extremely strong.

He stopped at the doorstep, which wasn't so much a doorstep as a congealed heap of all the cold

5

pig fat Uncle Vern had scraped out of the frying pan over the years.

Ned felt dizzy. He knew that dizziness could happen to people who didn't get enough fresh vegetables. Specially when they were short of sleep because of cold beds and noisy pigs who slurped tree mould all night. But Ned was pretty sure his dizziness was from something else.

The something that was in front of him.

Ned gaped.

Standing in the mud outside the hovel were six horses. Black ones. With silver plumes on their heads.

Behind them was a coach so golden and purple and gleaming that even a boy who'd never been to school knew instantly it was royal. Even before the two courtiers standing stiffly to attention bowed to him, opened the coach door, bowed to him again and murmured, 'Your Majesty'.

Ned had never been mistaken for a king before and it was making him feel a bit brain-addled himself. Which was why the coach journey was almost over before he realised his mistake.

Poop, thought Ned. Uncle Vern's right, I am a fool.

The only reason Ned had let the coach whisk him away, the only reason he hadn't explained to the courtiers that he was just the humble nephew of a mould farmer, was so he could get to the king and beg His Majesty to send a doctor with lots of strong acorns and leeches to cure Uncle Vern's brain.

Except, Ned now realised, Uncle Vern's brain didn't need curing. Because, unlike Ned, Uncle Vern wasn't brain-addled at all. This royal coach with its velvet cushions and silk curtains and delicate snacks on silver platters proved that.

The only brain-addled person, thought Ned, is whoever thinks I'm the king.

'Excuse me,' said Ned to the courtiers.

He wanted to explain his mistake and ask them to turn the coach round and take him home before he got into trouble for impersonating a monarch.

But the courtiers fell to their knees and held out the platters again.

Ned took one more quail drumstick and a couple more hummingbird nuggets, just to be polite. Plus, after two years of pig-nostril gruel, they were very delicious.

He ate them quickly so he could say what he had to say.

But by the time he'd finished chewing, the coach was clattering over a very large drawbridge and the courtiers were opening the curtains so Ned could see the majestic gleaming radiance of the royal castle.

Inside the castle walls, thousands of people stared at Ned. Well, hundreds, but when you lived in a hamlet with seven other peasants and eleven pigs, and the only time you had visitors was when the pigs had worms, even hundreds seemed scary.

Specially when they were all so well dressed. And kneeling down. And touching the muddy ground with their foreheads as you stepped out of the coach.

Well, not stepped.

Were carried.

'Your Majesty.'

The words rumbled around the huge castle courtyard in a mighty reverential whisper. Followed by a roar.

'The King Is Dead,' roared the crowd. 'Long Live The King.'

Oh, thought Ned. Uncle Vern was right about that too. I'd better get this whole misunderstanding cleared up.

Ned peered around the courtyard, trying to see who was in charge.

Whoever it was, he hoped they'd be wise and kind. The sort of viscount or bishop or admiral who understood that mistakes were sometimes made. And that a boy who made one or two of them shouldn't necessarily have his entrails boiled in oil.

'Sire.'

The two courtiers reverently placed Ned onto a red and gold carpet. But it wasn't the courtiers who had spoken.

Ned looked up.

Standing over him, bowing slightly, was the tallest man Ned had ever seen. He was very thin, but he must have been at least five foot six or even seven.

Amazing, thought Ned. People who don't live in bogs grow really tall. He could scrape the mould off a low branch without using a ladder.

'Welcome, Your Majesty,' said the man, and there was something about his haughty voice and dark pointy beard and the silver thread woven through his sumptuous clothes and the fur around the edge of his cloak and the jewels on the hilt of his sword and the way people lay down in the mud so he could walk on them without getting his boots dirty that made Ned think he might be the person in charge.

'On behalf of your worshipful subjects,' said the man, 'my humble greetings. I am your Lord Chamberlain, at Your Majesty's service.'

'Hello,' said Ned.

His voice came out squeaky, partly because of all the people listening, and partly because the Lord Chamberlain's eyes were making him feel nervous.

They were dark and darting and didn't look worshipful, humble or friendly.

'Actually,' stammered Ned, 'there's been a bit of a mistake.'

He was finding it hard to get words out, so he gestured towards the two courtiers from the coach. This would give the Lord Chamberlain an idea about the general nature of the mistake.

The Lord Chamberlain's eyes narrowed, which made them even scarier.

'A mistake?' he said.

Ned nodded.

'Please accept my apologies,' said the Lord Chamberlain. 'It won't happen again.'

Before Ned could say anything else, the Lord Chamberlain's sword flashed and the heads of the two courtiers plopped onto the ground, followed by the thud of their bodies.

Ned felt sick.

He decided to leave the topic of mistakes for a while, until he wasn't feeling so faint.

'What else does Your Majesty desire?' said the Lord Chamberlain.

'Can I sit down for a moment, please?' said Ned.

The royal throne was huge and uncomfortable. Ned's feet didn't even touch the ground, and jewels were poking him in several personal places.

He sipped the water he'd asked for.

The gold goblet was almost too heavy to lift, but at least the water didn't taste as though pigs had been washing in it.

Ned sighed.

He wanted to go home.

True, at home the water wasn't this clean and you had to drink it from the same mug as Uncle Vern. Verily, at home you didn't get to wear soft velvet robes like this, or real fur underwear. But at home you could be yourself and you were safe from murderous blades. Except when Uncle Vern was trimming pork giblets with a cleaver, but that wasn't often.

'Feeling better, Your Highness?'

Ned jumped.

The Lord Chamberlain had seated himself very close to Ned on a silver throne almost as big as the royal one.

Ned wasn't sure what to say.

A large number of other people were very close too. Courtiers mostly, anxiously hovering around with things a king might need, such as more gold goblets, whole roast oxen, maps of countries to invade, and great mounds of the exotic brightly coloured things Ned had heard about, called fruit.

The Lord Chamberlain stood up and clapped his hands.

The vast throne room emptied in a few seconds.

'Your Majesty,' said the Lord Chamberlain. 'My duty is to be your royal advisor, and my advice is that we should have a little chat.'

'Alright,' said Ned nervously.

'You are probably wondering, Your Most Royal Highness,' said the Lord Chamberlain, 'why you are the king.'

'Sort of,' said Ned.

'It's simple,' said the Lord Chamberlain. 'Your great-great-great-great-grandmother was a distant member of the royal family.'

Ned blinked with surprise.

'Well,' continued the Lord Chamberlain, 'she wasn't exactly a family member, but she used to remove worms from the royal hunting dogs and those dogs were so grateful they treated her just like family. Peed on her hovel, dug up her garden, they truly loved her. Which we calculate makes you one million four hundred and sixty-three thousand two hundred and ninety-seventh in line to the throne.'

Ned struggled to take this in. Before he could ask the obvious question, the Lord Chamberlain answered it.

'The other one million four hundred and sixty-three thousand two hundred and ninety-six weren't available,' he said. 'Plagues, wars, overseas holidays, you can't imagine how relieved we were to find you.'

Ned could imagine, but it wasn't as simple as that.

'What if I don't want to be king?' he said quietly. 'Do I have a choice?'

'Oh yes,' said the Lord Chamberlain. 'You most certainly do have a choice. You can choose to be the king, the most powerful person in the land whose every need, desire and whim is instantly satisfied and whose every law, command and proclamation is instantly obeyed. Or you can choose not to be the king, which means you're trespassing in the royal palace, an offence punishable by instant –'

The Lord Chamberlain drew his sword.

'I'll be the king,' said Ned.

'Wise choice, Your Highness,' said the Lord Chamberlain, putting his sword away.

Ned sagged miserably.

His head hurt. At first he thought it was the diamonds in his crown digging into his skull. But he realised it couldn't be that. The crown was too big so the royal housemaids had lined it with a couple of socks.

The Lord Chamberlain handed Ned a scroll of parchment covered in scrawly marks.

Ned wished he'd learned to read, but Uncle Vern had always said it was a waste of time given that pigs couldn't write.

'Our Constitution requires only two things of you, Your Highness,' said the Lord Chamberlain. 'One is that you behave like a king at all times, a special person of wealth, power and very white wrist ruffles so your loyal subjects can feel a glow of pride just thinking about you. The other is that you never leave the royal castle. We don't want you going outside like the last king and picking up some snotty peasant sniffle that turns fatal so we have to go through this whole tedious business all over again.'

Ned sagged even more.

Now he knew how the pigs at home felt, pampered with all the tree mould they could eat and all the lie-downs they fancied.

But utterly trapped.

The Lord Chamberlain was watching Ned closely again.

'As your royal advisor, Your Majesty,' he said, 'I advise you to make a start.'

Ned realised what the Lord Chamberlain meant.

Start behaving like a king.

Ned couldn't think of a single law, command or proclamation. He tried to summon up a need, desire or whim. Apart from going home, nothing.

The Lord Chamberlain's hand was resting on the hilt of his sword.

Ned suddenly remembered the anxious hovering courtiers and all the things they'd been offering him.

'Bring me a bandana,' he said in the most regal voice he could manage.

The Lord Chamberlain gave him a look.

'Your Highness wants a colourful scarf-like piece of fabric tied rakishly around his head? May I suggest that what Your Majesty wants is a banana.'

Ned sighed. It seemed he couldn't even get that right.

He wasn't a king, he was a fool.

Ned snuggled into the huge, soft, warm royal bed.

What a brilliant first command he'd finally come up with.

'I command,' he'd commanded, 'that I spend most of my time in bed.'

Nobody argued.

Maybe, Ned thought to himself, I'm going to be

quite a reasonably good king after all.

It was a magnificent bed, and easily big enough to hold all the things he might want to ask for.

So far there were just bananas. The first one had been so delicious, he'd asked for more. As the courtiers brought them in, the Lord Chamberlain explained that the bravest ships' captains in the land spent years on dangerous oceans to bring the bananas back from distant shores. By ancient royal command they sailed home the cold way, via the North Pole, so the bananas didn't get too ripe.

Ned was impressed.

He made a note to make sure his commands were that good.

The Lord Chamberlain also explained that a king shouldn't have to peel his own bananas, so they'd got him a trained chimp. Well, not a chimp exactly, but they'd found a very nimble-fingered monk with a protruding lower jaw.

Ned sighed contentedly. This was a wonderful experience, people being kind and considerate to him. The other people in his life had always been too busy for that, or too dead, and he was enjoying the feeling.

'Another banana please,' said Ned to the monk.

The monk got peeling.

'Your Majesty,' said the Lord Chamberlain, who was standing in the corner of the royal bedroom keeping an eye on things. 'You don't have to say please. You're the king.'

'Sorry,' said Ned.

'Or sorry,' said the Lord Chamberlain.

Ned covered his embarrassment by eating the banana.

He still had a bit to learn about being a king.

'I want to make a Royal Proclamation,' said Ned to the Lord Chamberlain.

The Lord Chamberlain raised an eyebrow.

Ned guessed why.

He'd been king for three days now and they'd both lost count of the bananas he'd eaten, and other fruit of all kinds, and vegetables and nuts except for acorns, and interesting colourful pork dishes from faraway lands.

But this was his first proclamation.

'I want to proclaim,' said Ned, 'that everybody in my kingdom be happy.'

Ned had been thinking about this all morning. He'd been thinking about how much power he had, which when he really thought about it was a humungous amount. He'd been thinking about how much good he could do with that power.

And suddenly it hit him.

He wanted everybody in his whole kingdom to be extremely happy.

'If I may advise Your Majesty,' said the Lord Chamberlain. 'A proclamation is a statement of how things are. If Your Highness wishes to proclaim universal happiness, what is required first are some means to make people happy. I suggest commands and laws, with the death penalty for people who don't obey them.'

Ned sighed.

With the Lord Chamberlain it was always the death penalty.

Ned could still hear scrubbing from the other side of the bed where the nimble-fingered monk was trying to get bloodstains out of the carpet after the Lord Chamberlain had beheaded a courtier who'd brought Ned a bruised apricot.

'Alright,' said Ned. 'Pass a law to make everyone happy.'

It was the Lord Chamberlain's turn to sigh.

'If I may advise Your Majesty,' he said. 'People may need a little more help than that.'

Good grief, thought Ned. Can't anyone think for themselves? Do I have to do everything around here?

'Alright,' he said. 'Law number one. Everybody must have enough to eat, including three types of fruit per week, two types of vegetable and at least one interesting colourful pork dish from a faraway land. Law number two . . .'

The Lord Chamberlain clapped his hands.

Several nervous courtiers came in with parchment, ink and quill pens.

For the rest of the afternoon, Ned made laws, the courtiers wrote them down, and the Lord Chamberlain frowned.

It was very hard work.

Ned needed a lot of strawberries and truffled pork ribs to keep his strength up.

The gentle chink of fine porcelain coaxed Ned out of his cosy slumber.

He opened his eyes.

At first he couldn't see where the sound was coming from. The bed was piled so high with buns that Ned took a few moments to spot the figure on the other side of the room holding a tray.

Was it another annoying courtier with yet another chamber pot?

No, it was a girl, a few years older than him.

He noticed how different she looked from the other females he'd seen in his weeks at the castle. She was wearing a simple white smock and apron, and her fair hair was tied back in a ponytail. She didn't have any of the ringlets or powder or lice that the other women wore in their hair.

'I'm Genevieve, Your Majesty,' she said, her eyes cast modestly downwards. 'I'll be serving you from now on.'

About time, thought Ned grumpily.

He'd issued the command to the Lord Chamberlain ages ago, before having his nap.

'No more courtiers,' he'd said. 'I'm sick of them flocking in here, bowing and scraping and leaving furrows in the carpet with their foreheads when they back out of the room.'

The Lord Chamberlain had seemed to agree. Possibly, Ned thought, because he'd had to behead several courtiers only that week for bringing Ned buns with thumb prints on them.

'From now on,' Ned had commanded the Lord Chamberlain, 'I only want to be served by one person.'

And here she was.

'What have you got for me?' said Ned, greedily eyeing the plates on Genevieve's tray.

'Lime and rose marmalade buns,' said Genevieve. 'Candied butterfly buns. Hazelnut and gold-leaf custard buns. And a new savoury bun that contains the stewed gizzards of some rare but delicious furry woodland creatures.'

'Yum,' said Ned. 'Give them here.'

With a regal wave of his hand he swept off the bed several dozen of the other types of buns he was already bored with. He grabbed the plate from Genevieve and started gobbling the new ones.

For a fleeting moment Ned remembered the taste of his very first bun. A simple warm yeasty ball of light-as-air dough with a bit of vanilla icing on top.

It had only been a few days ago that he'd proclaimed he was sick of fruit and meat, and a nervous courtier had appeared with his first bun on a tray, but it seemed like a lifetime.

Ned pushed another bun into his mouth and turned to Genevieve.

'You look like a reasonably intelligent person,' he said, spraying her with bits of hazelnut and gold leaf. 'What's the word from my kingdom? Are people happy yet?'

Genevieve glanced at the Lord Chamberlain, whose face stayed blank.

'Well, Your Majesty,' said Genevieve, 'it's early days yet. The Bedtime Story Law seems to be working quite well. And the Saying Please And Thank You Law seems to be very popular, except with Vikings and Goths. But the law requiring everyone to tell fifteen jokes a day is causing some difficulties. The murder rate is up alarmingly and people are saying they'd rather get the plague than hear another knock-knock joke.'

Ned scowled.

'Ungrateful scum,' he muttered. 'They're given the chance to be happy and they don't even take it. I'm working my fingers to the bun, I mean bone, for that selfish rabble. Maybe we should find a few of the really unhappy ones and make an example of them.'

Ned dragged a custardy finger across his own neck.

Genevieve glanced at the Lord Chamberlain again.

'It's an option,' said the Lord Chamberlain.

Ned opened his mouth to explain that he hadn't meant chop their heads off, he'd just meant make them uncomfortably sticky with custard. But he closed it again.

Sometimes a king had to be ruthless.

'Here,' said Genevieve. 'Let me clear away some of these stale buns.'

She made a small bag of her apron and started dropping buns into it one by one.

'Get rid of them all,' growled Ned, sweeping the remaining few hundred onto the floor. 'And tell those lazy curs in the kitchen that if they don't prepare fifty new types of bun by the morning, all delicious, I'll pass a Cooks Dangling Off The Battlements While Crows Peck Off Their Tummy Fat Law.'

Genevieve paused and furrowed her brow.

Then she leaned closer to Ned than any non-royal subject was meant to lean, including the Lord Chamberlain.

'Your Majesty,' she said quietly. 'You don't think being king is going to your head a bit, do you?'

She went back to picking up buns.

Ned stared at her.

He couldn't believe what she'd just said.

It was treason.

Didn't she realise that any second now the Lord Chamberlain would have his sword out and her head off?

Except that wasn't happening. The Lord Chamberlain was calmly watching as she calmly picked up buns.

Maybe the Lord Chamberlain didn't hear her, thought Ned. Or maybe I didn't hear her correctly.

Maybe she said something else. Or maybe she didn't say anything at all. Maybe I only thought she did.

But deep down Ned knew that she'd said it and he'd heard it.

And that there was one thing even a king couldn't banish.

The truth.

Ned closed his eyes and sank back onto his pillows. Several of which, he could feel, had buns stuffed inside them.

A tiny nagging thought started to form in the back of his mind, as far away as a jagged piece of crystalised ginger on top of a bun three pillows down, but just as impossible to ignore.

Maybe, he thought miserably, she's right.

Ned stared at the ceiling of the royal bedroom.

In the gloom of the early evening, he could just make out the unicorns and dragons on the royal crest, which was inlaid into the ceiling and was carved from rare timbers and mother-of-pearl and slices of the thigh bones of old enemies of the realm.

To Ned they looked like pigs dancing happily.

He couldn't stop thinking about what he'd left behind at home and how much he missed it.

Genevieve is right, he thought miserably.

Being king had gone to his head and he'd turned into a monster.

'Are you there, Lord Chamberlain?' said Ned.

There was no reply.

Ned couldn't see if the Lord Chamberlain was in his corner, or if he'd popped out to behead someone. The Lord Chamberlain was one of those people who could sleep standing up, Ned had seen it, but he always snored a bit and ground his teeth, and at the moment Ned couldn't hear either of those sounds.

Ned got out of bed.

His legs felt wobbly. Probably because he hadn't used them for several weeks, apart from kicking a few buns off the bed.

He headed for the door.

Wobbly or not, he had to do this. Apologise for his behaviour, starting with saying sorry to Genevieve, then the courtiers, then maybe even the Lord Chamberlain.

The corridor was very long.

Ned spotted a figure sitting on a bench against the wall in the distance. Some of the candles had blown out, and in the gloom Ned couldn't make out who it was.

As he got closer, he started to feel nervous.

What if it was one of the cooks, brooding about having to stay up all night inventing new buns. Pushed to the brink by exhaustion and custard fatigue. Desperate to use his knife on something more deserving than the internal organs of small furry forest creatures.

A power-crazed king, for example.

Ned shuddered.

The figure turned towards Ned and stood up.

Ned froze. He could see the silhouette of what the figure was holding. It looked like a huge knife. Ned turned to run. Then remembered he couldn't. He was wearing the royal nightgown, which was so big on him it flopped over his feet in folds.

'Ned?'

The figure had spoken. It spoke again, in a familiar voice.

'That nightgown's wa' too warm, lad. Ye'll be dyin' of infant mortality in that thing.'

'Uncle Vern,' shouted Ned, running towards him.

He tripped and fell into Uncle Vern's arms. They'd never actually hugged before, and it was a bit awkward at first, specially as Uncle Vern was also holding his pig-lard-shaping stick which he'd brought with him for self-defence. But they settled into it after a while and both enjoyed it.

'What are you doing here?' said Ned.

'I came to see you, bitty lad,' said Uncle Vern. 'Beseech ye to stop sendin' the trees.'

Ned stared at him, puzzled. Then remembered. Way back, in his first week as king, he'd issued a command that damp trees should be delivered to Uncle Vern in large numbers. The royal army had departed the same day to carry out the order.

'It were a nice thought, Your Highness,' said Uncle Vern nervously, and for a moment Ned thought he was going to prostrate himself on the floor. 'But them army lads planted 'em, and the forest got too big like. I was out there scrapin' last week and it took me two days to find my way home.'

'Sorry,' said Ned in a small voice. 'Being king went to my head.'

'Aye,' said Uncle Vern, putting a sympathetic hand on Ned's shoulder. 'That can happen.'

'How did you get in here?' said Ned.

'Bribed the guards wi' some pork chops,' said Uncle Vern. 'Then some Lord Chamberlain was about to remove my bonce, but the queen turned up and saved me.'

Ned stared at Uncle Vern.

'The queen?' he said.

'Aye,' said Uncle Vern. 'A slip of a girl, but nice.'

Ned felt faint.

'She's in there,' said Uncle Vern, pointing to a huge pair of doors. 'Welcoming guests at a royal ball or summat. But after that she said she'd take me to see you.'

Ned tried to speak, but all he could do was stand with his mouth open.

'Ye alright, lad?' said Uncle Vern. 'Ye be lookin' a bit like a brain-addled piglet.'

Things didn't improve for Ned when the doors of the royal ballroom swung open and light and noise and merriment spilled out, followed closely by a young woman in a dazzling ballgown and a mass of glittering diamonds and a crown.

Ned blinked.

It was Genevieve.

'It's alright, Your Highness,' said Uncle Vern to Genevieve. 'Ye don't have to trouble yerself. I've found him.'

Ned's mouth stayed open.

'Ned,' said Uncle Vern, 'this is Her Royal Highness Queen Genevieve as I was telling ye about.'

Ned tried to say something, but all that came out was a squeak.

'Poor Ned,' said Queen Genevieve, 'I owe you an apology. I'm afraid I've used you selfishly for my own purposes.'

Ned didn't understand what she meant, but he suddenly found he could speak, so he did.

'That's alright, I don't mind,' squeaked Ned. 'Your Highness.'

He wasn't sure if it was really alright, but what else could you say to a queen?

'I should explain,' said Queen Genevieve. 'As you know, my father the king died suddenly and I was crowned much earlier than I'd been expecting. So I decided to do what my grandfather did when he was crowned very young. Allow a young commoner to be king for a while and witness what happens to us all if we have too much power and aren't careful with it and start behaving like a power-mad froth-brain.'

Ned digested this, and the more he did, the more foolish he felt.

'I'm sorry to have deceived you, Ned,' said Queen Genevieve. 'But you have done me a great service. Throughout my reign, if ever I feel power going to my head, I'll think of you.'

'That be nice, ent it, Ned?' said Uncle Vern.

Ned didn't think it was nice at all. He wanted to crawl under a large stone for ever.

'I can see you have mixed feelings about this, Ned,' said Queen Genevieve. 'I'm sorry.'

'I don't have mixed feelings, Your Highness,' said Ned. 'I have very clear feelings. I'm a fool.'

'No, Ned,' said Queen Genevieve, 'you're not a fool. You're a Fool, and that's a very different thing.'

Ned didn't have a clue what she was talking about.

'A Fool,' said Queen Genevieve, 'is a very important person in a royal household. He's the person who, if the monarch is in danger of turning into a power-crazed dunce, says or does something to bring that monarch to their senses. Just like you've done for me these past few weeks.'

'I'll be a pig's nostril,' said Uncle Vern.

Even though Ned was still stunned, he could see the sense in what the queen was saying.

'Ned,' said Queen Genevieve, 'I'm going to reign for a long time if I can stop peasants sneezing on me. The longer I have absolute power, the greater the risk I'll turn into an addled-headed twit. So I very much need a Fool, and I'd like it to be you. It's a very well-paid job. I do hope you'll accept.'

* * *

Ned did accept.

People had been calling him a fool for so long that it was an easy decision to make. Except, as he quickly discovered, the Queen was right. This was very different.

It was hard work, but very satisfying.

The Queen got a bit tetchy with him at times, but that's when he knew he was doing his job well. Other times he could see in her eyes how much she valued him.

There were times when it almost felt like he was running the country. That's when he needed somebody to take him down a peg or two, and luckily he had someone.

Uncle Vern, the new Lord Chamberlain.

'I'ope them pigs is alright,' Uncle Vern would sometimes say.

'Don't fret, Lord Chamberlain,' Queen Genevieve would say. 'The old Lord Chamberlain was born to farm pigs. When slaughter time comes, he'll have their heads off and they won't feel a thing.'

Sometimes Ned did feel a little sorry for the old Lord Chamberlain, having to scrape damp trees with such a fine sword. But at least he had plenty of trees to scrape.

'That's as maybe,' Uncle Vern would reply. 'But them pigs'll be missin' Ned summat rotten. He has a way with them pigs, does young Ned, specially when their nostrils gets blocked.'

And Ned would give a small smile, partly from

the fond memories, and partly because he knew how lucky he was to have Uncle Vern.

With Uncle Vern around, there was no chance of a young man getting full of himself and ending up with a head like a custard bun. A big one with silly gold leaf on top.

And that's just how Ned wanted it.

I might be a Fool, he thought happily, but I'm not a fool.

Troll

'Look at that,' says Gavin, putting his hot chocolate down and tapping the screen of his tablet indignantly.

None of us look.

We're not being rude. We like Gavin a lot. But getting indignant is Gavin's hobby. And when he says 'look at that', he doesn't really want anybody to actually look.

Gavin's a good step-dad and we're glad he's got a hobby he enjoys. He spends hours each evening flicking around the news sites on his tablet, looking for things to make him feel indignant and stunned and outraged by what people get up to.

He loves it. He likes nothing better than finding something that makes his voice go squeaky with indignation.

'Look at that,' he says again, his voice squeaky with indignation.

We still don't look.

Mum stays dozing on the settee in front of the TV because that's her hobby.

I stay on the floor sending texts because that's my hobby. Well, not so much a hobby. I've got several friends whose lives would be a total mess without advice from me, so it's more of a job except I don't get paid.

Trump our dog stays on the floor next to me licking his bottom, which is his hobby. Like Gavin, he doesn't expect other people to do his hobby either.

'Look at that,' says Gavin for the third time. He usually says it three times.

We still don't look because we know he'll tell us about it.

'This report here in the *Guardian*,' says Gavin. 'It's about a nun helping injured children. She's devoted her life to setting up a clinic in Miami to treat children with serious head injuries.'

'Mmmm,' says Mum in the tone she always uses, the one that means 'that's terrible'.

'Exactly,' says Gavin. 'They mostly get the head injuries from walking into things while they're looking at their phones.'

You've got to hand it to Gavin. Most of the things that get him worked up are pretty interesting.

Except it turns out that this time it isn't the phones that have got him indignant. Or the children.

'As you'd expect,' says Gavin, 'the comments are

mostly nice ones about the nun. *God bless you, sister.*
Stuff like that. But look what some miserable, sour-
minded troll has written. *You smell, fat bum.*'

Suddenly I'm not smiling.

I go over and look at Gavin's screen.

Oh no.

I'm shocked, and I can see Gavin is too. Though
his shock might mostly be because I've actually
come over for a look.

I'm feeling shocked for another reason. And
horrified. But not by the comment on the screen.
By the username.

Beansprout.

He's at it again.

'Trolling a nun,' says Gavin. 'It's a sick world.'

I go back to my spot on the floor, trying not to
show how I'm feeling. I casually send a message on
my phone to the friend I was giving advice to before
this happened.

*Sorry, family emergency. If the vinegar doesn't
work, try the hair dryer. Don't squeeze them. Catch
you later.*

Then I casually get to my feet and head towards
the door.

'Back in a sec,' I say.

The others don't even look up from their
hobbies.

I sprint down the hallway to Nate's room.
I don't check if his door's unlocked. It won't be.
I give it several thumps.

33

'Nate,' I hiss. 'You're gunna be in big trouble if you don't stop that right now. Let me in.'

A long silence.

Then Nate's voice. 'Go away.'

'Open this door,' I say, 'or I'll unscrew the lock.'

He knows I could. His history project in term three was on convicts and I helped him make convict chains out of Mum's metallic link belt and the lock from the shed door.

I listen, trying to tell if he's coming to open his door.

He's on his feet, I can hear him. It sounds as though he's moving things around. If he's trying to hide his computer, that's stupid. We all know he's got it. Gavin bought it for him to do his homework.

What a mistake that was.

The door opens. Nate glares at me.

'What?' he says.

He knows what. I steer him back into the room and close the door behind us.

'You said you'd stop,' I say.

'Stop what?' says Nate, his blond curls flopping into his eyes which he does when he wants to look innocent.

'This,' I say, stepping over to his computer which is still on his desk and still switched on.

I peer at the screen and see that Nate's been looking at a YouTube video of an Olympic weight lifter. There's a list of comments under it. The last comment is from Beansprout.

You're weak.

I click into the computer's history.

More comments under a cute cat photo.

Beansprout: *You're ugly.*

Click. The Prime Minister talking about bilateral free-trade negotiations.

Beansprout: *You're stupid.*

Click. A news report about sick kids in Finland.

Beansprout: *You're Finished.*

I turn and give Nate a look.

'It's my hobby,' he says quietly.

I sigh. Poor kid. In a way I don't blame him, but I can't tell him that. If Mum finds out what he's doing she'll go ballistic.

'It's alright for you,' says Nate. 'You and Mum and Gavin have all got your hobbies.'

'I don't call this a hobby,' I say. 'Adding to the anger and unhappiness and bad feeling in the world.'

'It's what Dad does,' mumbles Nate.

He looks so sad I want to hug him.

Instead I grab his shoulders.

'Dad's got his own shock-jock radio show,' I say. 'Adding to the anger and unhappiness and bad feeling in the world is his job. You're a nice kid who's not on the radio, so stop being a troll.'

'I'm not a troll,' says Nate.

'Yes you are,' I say.

'You don't know anything about trolls,' says Nate.

I'm about to say 'I know a troll when I see one', but I'm distracted by a noise from inside Nate's wardrobe.

Two noises. A thump and a snort.

'What was that?' I say.

'Nothing,' says Nate too quickly.

There's another snorting sound from inside the wardrobe.

I step over and open the wardrobe door.

I don't know what I was expecting to see in there. A schoolmate, maybe. Or Nate's iPod running a podcast of Dad's radio show, which Nate secretly listens to sometimes.

But not this.

'Get lost, big nose,' growls a raspy voice. 'This is flosshead's room.'

For a second I think it's some sort of animatronic toy. An amazingly lifelike robot, waist-high with dirty green rubbery skin and about sixteen batteries.

But when it rolls its eyes at me and screws up its snout and then snorts again and strings of snot flop onto the floor, I know it's a living creature.

'Are you deaf,' it rasps, 'as well as thick as a toilet roll?'

I don't reply. Just sort of gape.

'You can stand there with your stupid mouth open all week,' says the creature. 'I'm not throwing you any fish.'

I turn to Nate. I still can't speak, but I can see he's imagining the questions I'd be asking if I could.

'I told you I'm not a troll,' says Nate quietly. 'This is a troll.'

'Mr Troll to you, toilet brush,' says the troll.

'Where did it come from?' I squeak, my voice suddenly back.

'It climbed in through the window about two weeks ago,' says Nate.

I stare at them both. Two weeks? No wonder Nate's been keeping his door locked so much lately.

'Dropped in to visit a workmate,' says the troll. 'But the flabby big-mouth's done a runner.'

Does he mean Dad?

Must do, the rest of us are still here.

Which is gobsmacking. We've met some pretty horrible friends of Dad's, but nothing like this.

I start to ask the troll how long he's known my father, then stop myself. I must still be in shock. Only people in shock would try to have a normal conversation with a creature that could be from outer space for all I know.

'W-where are you from?' I stammer to the troll.

'Adelaide,' says the troll. 'At least, that's where my last job was. Insult adviser to some meathead in the state government. Got bored. Same old crapola. There's thousands of us trolls in this country and most of us work in politics. I fancied going back to radio for a bit. Not that it's any of your business, mudflap features.'

'He's been helping me with my hobby,' says Nate.

'Helping you?' sneers the troll. 'Get real. You

haven't written a word, fluffhead. All you're good for is scraping the dog's bum.'

'He likes dog poo,' says Nate. 'On cracker biscuits.'

I stare at Nate again. That explains the smell in his room, and why there's never any cracker biscuits when I get home from school.

I turn back to the troll.

'Well that's all over now,' I say. 'You're leaving.'

The troll gives a snort and another blob of something stringy flops onto Nate's carpet.

'I'll leave when I want to, darling,' says the troll.

I see red. We'll have to clean that carpet now. And nobody with yellow teeth calls me darling unless I let them.

I pick up the troll.

He's heavy, but no heavier than a big plastic garbage bag full of garbage.

'OK, Mr Garbage Bag,' I say. 'Listen carefully. We've got friends up north. Last visit they showed me how they kill cane toads. Lots of salt, then into the freezer. If the toads struggle on the way to the kitchen, sometimes a cricket bat is used. Nate, grab your cricket bat.'

Nate doesn't move. He's staring open-mouthed at me and the troll.

'Now,' I say.

Nate grabs the cricket bat.

The troll is swearing at me and spraying me with stringy stuff, but I don't let that distract me.

'So,' I say to the troll, 'here's your choice. Go now, or we'll be paying a visit to the spare freezer in the garage.'

I carry the frothing troll over to the window.

'Open it, Nate,' I say.

Nate opens the window.

I throw the troll out.

He lands on his head on the lawn, scrambles to his feet and yells at me.

'Interfering cow,' he splutters.

'It's my hobby,' I say.

The troll takes a couple of steps towards me.

I take the cricket bat from Nate and grip it in both hands.

The troll stops and snorts again.

'I'm done with you dopey frothheads anyway,' he says. 'I've got more important things to do. Policy adviser to the education minister probably, so I can get your school shut down.'

Muttering, the troll stomps away into the night.

I close the window.

Nate is looking at me like he thinks I'm going to yell at him.

I don't.

'Let's sit down and have a chat,' I say.

'Don't want to,' says Nate.

'If you really want to get Dad's attention,' I say, 'I can tell you a better way of doing it.'

Nate sits down and we have a chat.

* * *

That was a month ago.

Things have been very different since.

For some of us, anyway. My friends are still mostly disasters and I still have to put in overtime to stop them ruining their lives and their skin.

Mum has started helping me, which is great. She knows some great healing ointments and natural moisturisers for people who've tried to get rid of pimples with a nail file.

I still have to spend a lot of time on the floor with my phone, which is what I'm doing now.

Gavin still spends a lot of time being indignant, which is what he's doing now.

'Look at this,' he says indignantly, putting his hot chocolate down and tapping the screen of his tablet.

Nate goes over and has a look.

For a moment Gavin looks pleased, which is one of the things that are different now.

Then he goes back to being indignant.

'More state schools being closed down,' he says. 'And at the same time they're giving more cash to private schools.'

Nate nods thoughtfully.

'Probably be closing ours next,' he says.

'Exactly,' says Gavin. 'Elitist mongrels.'

Nate thinks some more.

'Why don't we write a letter?' he says to Gavin. 'To the education minister. Explain to him in simple words why this'll harm the future of our country.

We'll put it on your Facebook again. That letter we wrote last week to the health minister got twenty-seven thousand likes.'

'OK,' says Gavin to Nate. 'Let's do it.'

I smile, in a relieved sort of way.

It was a risk, but I'm glad it's working out. Anyone can be a troll, look at Dad. But our world needs us to use our hearts and brains instead of our spleens and bile and other stringy bits.

I said this to Mum the other day.

She agreed.

'All our futures depend on it,' she said.

She paused and smiled.

'Plus,' she said, 'it's so nice to see Gavin finally sharing his hobby.'

The FDC

Archie wanted to go home, but he couldn't.

There was too much blood.

It was dripping through his fingers. If he didn't do something fast, his school uniform would look like a year-one art project.

An elderly man walking past gave Archie a sympathetic nod.

'I had nosebleeds when I was a lad,' said the man. 'Frozen peas, that's what you need.'

Archie didn't reply. He kept his hands over his nose and gave the man a grateful look.

I need more than frozen peas, thought Archie. A bag of frozen pineapples would be better. Then next time Rosco Kruger picks on me, I can flatten him with them.

Trying not to drip too much, Archie hurried into the kids' playground behind the public library. He went over to the rubbish bin next to the monkey bars. The only useful thing he could see in the bin was a half-eaten Big Mac. He kept one hand on his nose and with the other he squished bits of the bun into two balls and stuffed them into his nostrils.

The blood stopped. For now.

Archie glanced around. At least the playground was empty. At least he didn't have to put up with little kids pointing at him and saying 'Mum, why has that boy got a bun up his nose?'

Archie wondered if his nose was bent. It felt bent. Rosco Kruger always twisted it hard, but today he'd twisted it extra hard.

That's all Mum and Dad need now, thought Archie. The expense of nose surgery on top of everything else.

He peered at his reflection in the shiny metal rubbish bin. His nose looked swollen but not bent or broken.

Archie waggled it cautiously.

Pain flashed through his head. So did a jolt of anger.

That vicious bully.

If there was any justice in the world, Rosco Kruger would be hanging upside down from these monkey bars now with the chains from the swings wrapped tight around his body, sobbing about how sorry he was while Archie stuffed McDonald's buns up his bully-boy nose till his head exploded.

Calm down, Archie told himself. Violent acts of revenge only happen in movies.

Mum was always saying that. Just like Dad was always saying how sometimes life does a poo on your head and you just have to wear it.

Archie sighed.

The bun balls were starting to feel like quarter pounders. Carefully Archie unplugged his nose. He waited a while to make sure the bleeding had stopped, then scuffed a hole in the ground and buried the bun balls hygienically under the slide.

He decided not to go home yet.

Best give the swelling a chance to go down.

Archie headed towards the library, trying not to think about what a happy place this playground had been for him and Mum and Dad before all their problems started.

As he passed the adventure sandpit, he noticed a red blob on one of the white-painted car tyres.

Oops, he thought. That was probably me.

Archie crouched down, spat on the dried blood and rubbed at it with the strap of his school bag. He didn't want hungry dogs licking the tyre and developing a taste for them and then chasing cars and getting run over.

The blood was really dried on.

He rubbed it as hard as he could.

'G'day,' said a gruff voice behind him.

Archie turned and peered up.

A large bloke in a work singlet and shorts was standing there, holding out his hand as if he wanted to shake.

Archie stood up nervously. Mum and Dad were always warning him to be careful of strangers.

'You're probably wondering who I am,' said the bloke.

No I'm not, thought Archie, but he didn't say that. He just gave a shrug, which he hoped made him look not that interested without being rude.

'I'm your FDC,' said the bloke.

Archie tried to work out what that meant. FDC?

'Fairy Demolition Contractor,' said the bloke.

Archie stared at him.

'I'm sort of like a fairy godmother,' said the bloke. 'Except I demolish things.'

Archie took a step back. Mum and Dad had warned him to be very careful of strangers like this. Ones with sad mental conditions who'd been released into the community without adequate medical support.

The bloke grinned.

'Dunno what I'm talking about, do you?' he said.

Archie shook his head. He wished his school bag was over his shoulder instead of on the ground behind the poor unfortunate deranged person. Then he could run.

'It's simple,' said the bloke. 'Everyone's got a fairy somebody.'

Archie didn't say anything.

Best not to encourage him.

'Which you probably didn't know,' continued the bloke, 'cause you've never met me before. We only turn up when you really really need us. Then you get your three wishes.'

Archie wondered if he should offer to go to the chemist and fetch some medication.

'With me you get three demolitions,' said the bloke. 'You choose three buildings, I knock 'em down.'

Or food, thought Archie. If there's any more McDonald's in the bin, I could distract him with that.

'We can start now, if you like,' said the bloke. 'I've got the rig with me.'

He pointed to something over Archie's shoulder.

Archie turned.

And almost fainted.

Behind him, parked in the library carpark, was a huge semi-trailer with a massive crane on the back. Hanging from the crane was a giant metal ball.

Archie sat down on the roundabout. It wasn't moving, but he felt like everything else was whirling around.

'I've got explosives in the truck,' said the bloke. 'And a sledgehammer for small jobs. You choose.'

Archie struggled to get his thoughts straight.

Would a sick person in the grip of a tragic fantasy actually have a truck like this? With a metal ball this size?

Archie didn't think so.

Perhaps it's me, he thought. Perhaps I'm hallucinating from loss of blood.

'I can see you're having a bit of trouble digesting it all,' said the bloke. 'What say we get started on the first one, so you can see how it works.'

Archie waggled his nose again.

Pain, just like before. Real pain, which meant this was almost certainly really happening.

Most of Archie still wanted to run, but part of him was beginning to feel a tiny bit curious.

Alright, very curious.

'What'll it be?' said the bloke. 'Flatten an old shed? Knock your school down? How about Parliament house? Wouldn't mind giving those mongrels a shake-up.'

Archie's mind was racing.

'By the way,' said the bloke, 'the name's Noel.'

He held out his hand again. Archie shook it cautiously. It was a big muscly hand with ginger hair on the back. Warm and solid.

It felt completely real.

Archie let go of Noel's hand and sat there for a few moments, waiting for a very strong feeling to leave him.

It didn't.

He looked up at Noel's big weatherbeaten face.

'Do you do violent acts of revenge?' he asked.

The Krugers' place was a big two-storey house in a posh street.

At one side of the house, next to the swimming pool, was Rosco's cubby.

Gang headquarters, that's what Rosco called it. But Archie knew a cubby when he saw one, even when it had gang members in it.

Archie could see the shadowy shapes through the cubby window as he peered out from his hiding place inside the front hedge. He could also see Noel's huge truck and gigantic wrecking ball filling up most of the Krugers' driveway.

Mr Kruger was coming out of the house, looking bewildered.

'What's going on?' he demanded.

Noel wound his window down.

'I'm here to demolish the cubby,' he said. 'Mind yourself.'

Mr Kruger stared up at him, dumbfounded.

Noel revved the huge engine and drove through a fence and across several flower beds and parked next to the swimming pool.

Mr Kruger yelled angrily.

'You can't do that!'

Somebody else screamed. It was Mrs Kruger, coming out of the house with a small dog and a terrified expression.

On the semi-trailer, winch motors howled and the giant metal ball started to move.

Archie tried to yell at Rosco to get out. But his voice was in shock. All he could do was croak, and that was muffled by the hedge and drowned out by the grinding of heavy machinery.

'Rosco,' yelled Mr Kruger.

Rosco's face appeared at the cubby window. He looked up at the metal ball and his mouth fell open.

The two gang members scrambled out of the cubby. Rosco followed, frantically trying to push them out of his way. One of the gang members fell into the pool.

Archie held his breath as the metal ball whooshed down. It hurtled over Rosco's head and smashed into the cubby.

Fragments of gaily painted wood and brick-textured plastic were flung across the garden, slicing the heads off flowers and shredding the washing on the line.

For a moment everything went quiet, except for the sound of a heavy-gauge chain being rewound into its storage position.

Archie realised his hands were hurting from gripping the hedge.

Rosco looked as stunned as if the metal ball had hit him. So did his parents and the gang members.

While Mr and Mrs Kruger dragged the dripping boy out of the pool, Rosco stared at his own wet clothes.

From the miserable expression on Rosco's face, Archie could see that the big wet patch on Rosco's pants hadn't come from the pool.

Noel was whistling an Abba tune as he backed the truck out into the street. He stopped next to Archie and held something out of the driver's window for Archie to take.

'When you're ready for your other two,' said Noel, 'ring this number.'

It was a business card.

Noel Watson, it said. *Demolition Contractor (Fairy).* And a very long phone number. Heaps of digits.

Archie didn't count them.

He was too busy diving back into the hedge as Mr and Mrs Kruger sprinted out of the garden after Noel's truck.

And too busy watching them come back in a daze because when they'd got round the corner, the truck had vanished.

'Mum,' said Archie in a small voice. 'Can I ask you something?'

Archie hated disturbing Mum while she was doing her paperwork. She needed all her energy and concentration for the letters she got back from the insurance company. For swearing at them and wheeling herself up and down the backyard till she'd calmed down.

But this was urgent.

'Course you can, love,' said Mum. She swung her wheelchair round to face him. 'What is it?'

Archie took a deep breath.

'Do you believe . . .?'

He couldn't say it.

Mum looked at him, concerned.

Archie blurted it out.

51

'Do you believe in fairies?'

Even as he heard himself say the words he knew it was a dopey question to ask a woman whose whole life had been ruined by a harsh world.

Except Mum didn't look like it was a dopey question. She was staring at him with a strange expression, concerned but sort of fascinated, and Archie was pretty sure it wasn't because his nose was still swollen.

'Has yours come?' she said quietly.

Archie stared at her.

She sounded like she'd almost been expecting this to happen.

Archie felt a bit faint. All he could do was nod.

'No details,' said Mum quickly. 'Don't tell me any details. This has to be your secret. You mustn't ever say who your fairy person is or what he or she does.'

Archie sat down on the settee. He could barely take this in. *Your fairy person?* Did that mean that everyone had a . . .?

Dad came in from the kitchen. He and Mum swapped a look.

Mum gave him a nod.

Dad blew out his cheeks. He sat down next to Archie and gave Archie's shoulder a squeeze.

'It's a shock, isn't it, mate?' he said. 'It is for all of us when we first find out. But it has to be a secret, son. Between you and your fairy whatever. If you break the secret, they go and they don't come back.'

Archie managed to find his voice.

'Does everybody have one?' he said.

Mum and Dad nodded.

'Everybody in the world?' said Archie.

'Sooner or later,' said Dad.

Archie felt like he was back on the roundabout.

'Are you OK, love?' said Mum.

'I think so,' said Archie, hoping he wouldn't faint or throw up from the shock. 'Why didn't you tell me? When you told me where babies come from, you could have tacked it on the end.'

Mum and Dad both sighed.

'All the parenting experts say it's best not to tell,' said Dad. 'Otherwise kids'll waste their childhoods wondering when their fairy person is going to turn up.'

Archie thought about this. He could sort of see the sense in it.

Sort of.

'Plus,' said Mum, 'some fairy experts reckon that knowing in advance, you run the risk of wasting your three wishes. Letting little problems get on top of you. So your fairy person appears too early and you use up your wishes before you really need them.'

Archie saw Mum and Dad give each other a sad glance.

He stared at them.

'Is that what happened to you?' he said.

They both nodded.

'I got a Fairy Chef,' said Mum quietly. 'Dad was up for a promotion at work and his boss was coming here for dinner and I was desperately worried that I wouldn't impress him with the meal. Then Marco appeared. Three delicious courses.'

She shook her head sadly.

Archie looked at Dad.

'Fairy Golf Instructor,' said Dad miserably. 'When I got the promotion, they told me I had to join the golf club, same as the other managers. What a waste. I only won the first three holes.'

Archie gave Mum and Dad a hug each. He knew exactly why they were so miserable. How awful it must be, to have used up all your wishes before the really bad things happened.

Mum and Dad were both looking at him.

Archie wanted to tell them that he wasn't going to waste his wishes. He was going to make the most of his. He was going to use his to bring a smile back to both their faces.

He was about to tell them how, then he remembered the rules.

So he kept quiet.

This was between him and his Fairy Demolition Contractor.

Archie stared up at the building. He'd forgotten it was this tall.

Eighty-six storeys.

Could Noel manage eighty-six storeys?

'G'day, Arch,' said Noel's voice behind him.

Archie jumped and turned round. Noel was standing at the kerb in front of his truck.

Amazing. He'd only rung Noel two minutes ago. And two minutes ago there hadn't been a single parking spot available.

'This one here, is it?' said Noel, squinting up at the insurance company building.

Archie nodded, trying to look more determined than he suddenly felt.

'Right-oh,' said Noel. 'Better stand back a bit. Next street might be best.'

Archie didn't move as Noel heaved himself up into the cabin of the semi-trailer. The winch motors started whining and the chain started clanking.

'Wait,' yelled Archie.

The winch and the chain went silent. Noel leaned out of the driver's window.

'What is it, boss?' he said to Archie.

Archie tried to look like a boss. Like he wasn't having doubts.

Which he wasn't. Not really. It was just the people coming in and out of the building. People with their breakfast and their phones and their friends.

Ordinary people.

'No rush,' said Noel. 'Couple of minutes if you like. You probably want to take some photos, right? Before and after.'

Archie didn't want to take photos.

He had all the images he needed in his memory. Images of Mum's and Dad's sad and anguished faces.

Archie stared up at the top floors of the tower. On those floors, in those offices, the people weren't ordinary. They were the monsters who'd ruined Mum's and Dad's lives.

The insurance company managers.

'Just say the word,' called Noel from the cabin, 'and we'll get this one knocked over by morning tea.'

Archie clenched his teeth and kept staring up at the top of the building. He imagined the faces of the insurance company monsters when they realised their luxury offices didn't have floors any more. He imagined their screams as they plummeted down, surrounded by disintegrating concrete and other howling managers. He imagined the hundreds of other employees on the floors below, all plummeting too. All crashing down onto the people visiting the building, like this lady just going in with a toddler in a stroller.

He turned away.

'Right to go?' called Noel.

Archie looked up at his Fairy Demolition Contractor.

'Noel,' he said. 'Can I have a word please?'

The inside of the Noel's cabin didn't seem very luxurious for a fairy workplace. The vinyl on the seats was cracked and the whole cabin smelled of chips.

Archie only noticed this once he'd stopped talking and was waiting anxiously for Noel to reply.

Noel was frowning, perplexed.

'Never been asked that before,' he said. 'Just the top three floors? That's all?'

Archie nodded.

Noel rubbed his stubbly chin, still frowning.

'Nah,' he said. 'Sorry. Can't do it.'

Archie didn't understand. Before, when he was telling Noel the terrible story of what the insurance company did to Mum, how they'd refused to pay for the special operation that could have got her walking again, Noel had been outraged.

'The slimy mongrels,' Noel had said. 'If some maniac chucks a rock off a freeway footbridge and smashes your car windscreen and you stop and get out and another rock hits you, that's a car accident as far as I'm concerned, end of story. Only a slimy mongrel would quibble about that.'

And when Archie had told Noel how Dad, who worked for the insurance company, had tried to stand up for Mum and had been fired on the spot, Noel was outraged.

'Don't quote me on this,' he'd said, 'because I'm just a Fairy Demolition Contractor not a Fairy Hit Man, but those scumbags deserve to be whacked.'

Archie had been pleased to hear it.

So why had Noel gone all doubtful just because Archie didn't think the bottom eighty-three storeys deserved to be whacked?

'It's structural,' said Noel. 'To whack the top bit, you have to whack the bottom bit. The crane won't reach past the eleventh floor.'

Archie couldn't argue with that.

He looked out the window and saw the lady with the toddler leaving the building. He wondered if they were the family of one of the monster managers. Even if they were, did they deserve to be whacked?

'Do the lot, then, eh?' said Noel.

Archie struggled to give Noel the go-ahead.

He couldn't.

'What about all the innocent people?' he said.

Noel shrugged.

'I'm just a demolition contractor,' he said. 'Not a philosopher.'

'I'm not a philosopher either,' said Archie. 'But it doesn't seem right, whacking innocent people.'

Noel gave a long sigh.

'Sorry, Noel,' said Archie. 'Sorry I dragged you out for nothing.'

'You didn't,' said Noel. 'See, there's a rule. Once you make the call, I have to knock something down.'

Archie stared at Noel.

Noel shrugged apologetically.

Somebody tapped on the cabin door.

'Jeez,' said Noel, suddenly rigid with alarm. 'If that's a Fairy Inspector, I'm dead meat. Duck down, I'm not supposed to have clients in the cabin. Haven't got the insurance cover.'

The knock came again, louder.

Looking ashen, Noel slowly opened the cabin door.

Standing there, blinking up at them nervously, was Rosco Kruger.

'Hi Archie,' said Rosco. 'Sorry to disturb you.'

Archie stared.

'How did you know I was here?' he said to Rosco.

'I saw you hiding in the hedge yesterday,' said Rosco, 'after my cubby got demolished. And I came to see you this morning at your place. As I was arriving you were leaving, so I followed you here hoping you were coming to see . . . him.'

'The name's Noel,' said Noel gruffly.

He'd obviously decided Rosco wasn't a Fairy Inspector.

'What do you want?' said Archie.

Rosco didn't reply at first, just took several deep breaths.

While he was doing that, Archie had a sudden thought. If he told Rosco all about Noel now, his name, what he did, what he'd done to Rosco's cubby, then Noel would have to immediately disappear forever and nothing else would need to be demolished.

Except, Archie remembered with dismay, Rosco already knew all that.

Archie tried desperately to think of something he could tell Rosco about Noel that Rosco didn't know.

Before he could, Noel gave an exasperated snort.

'We're busy people here,' he said to Rosco. 'What do you want?'

Rosco took one more big breath and spoke up.

'I want you to demolish our house,' he said.

The big metal ball smashed through the upstairs of the Kruger house, hurling handmade convict bricks, chunks of high-quality plaster, slivers of Italian bathroom tile and bits of genuine roofing slate across the garden like shrapnel, where they made a complete mess of the Balinese gazebo.

'Yippee,' squealed Rosco, jiggling up and down and clapping his hands. 'I've wanted this for ages. My Fairy Sports Coach was hopeless. Get good at squash, he said. Win tournaments. Make your parents notice you. Make them as proud of you as they are of their house.'

Rosco suddenly scowled.

'As if,' he said.

Archie looked anxiously at the disintegrating house.

'You're totally sure your parents aren't in there?' he said to Rosco.

'I told you,' said Rosco. 'My mother's at the designer lighting shop and my father's at the art dealer's. As usual.'

Archie saw that neighbours were starting to assemble along the front fence. He could hear the distant sound of a police siren, coming closer.

Rosco gave the neighbours a glance.

'Don't worry,' he said to Archie. 'My parents spend their whole time re-decorating the house. People'll think they've just decided to go one step further.'

The big metal ball smashed into one of the downstairs rooms. Fragments of antique furniture, sections of lime-bleached floorboards, parts of designer lamps and bits of genuine original oil paintings flew across the lawns.

Archie could hear the police siren getting closer.

'Arch,' called Noel from the cab of the truck. 'You'd better pop off home. I'll finish up here. Been nice working with you.'

He gave Archie a wave.

Archie waved back, said thank you to Noel one last time, and turned to head home.

Rosco blocked his way. And grabbed him. Not by the nose this time. By the hand.

'Thanks for saving my family,' Roscoe said to Archie, shaking his hand emotionally. 'When I get a new gang headquarters, you're invited.'

Mum and Dad were both watching the TV news when Archie came in.

On the screen was the Kruger house. Which was strewn all over the Kruger garden. Neighbours and police and State Emergency Service teams were milling around.

Mum and Dad looked at Archie.

'That's the Kruger place,' said Dad.

'Rosco Kruger,' said Mum. 'Isn't he the boy who's been bullying you?'

Archie didn't know what to say.

'You don't have to say anything,' said Dad gently. 'That's the deal, remember.'

Archie did want to say something.

'Mine was a Fairy Demolition Contractor,' he said.

Mum and Dad both nodded slowly, as if they weren't surprised to hear this given what they'd just seen on the news.

Archie saw they were trying not to show their feelings, which didn't look like very happy ones.

'I suppose Rosco Kruger deserved it,' said Dad. 'But still, to knock his whole house down . . .'

'No Dad,' said Archie quietly. 'The bullying wasn't why Rosco's house got knocked down. His cubby, yes, but not the house.'

Mum and Dad weren't hiding their feelings now. They were both looking very puzzled.

'Rosco wanted the house knocked down,' explained Archie. 'His parents were so obsessed with it, they didn't have any time for him. I reckon that's why he bullied me. He was jealous of what great loving parents I've got.'

Mum and Dad swapped a glance.

'So even though Rosco had hurt you, you gave him one of your three wishes?' said Mum.

'I gave him two,' said Archie. 'His dad's a workaholic. Prefers a car dealership to his own son.'

Archie pointed to the TV screen, where the news reporter was standing in front of the wreckage of a car sales yard.

Mum and Dad swapped another look.

Archie was pretty sure he knew what they were thinking. This was the moment he'd been dreading. Having to confess and tell them the truth. That he hadn't been able to do the most important demolition of all.

'I'm sorry,' he said to them. 'Noel and me went to the insurance building and . . . I tried, I really did, for both of you, but . . .'

Archie could hear how small and sad his voice had got.

'But it was full of people,' he whispered. 'I'm sorry.'

He felt even worse now that Mum was reaching for a tissue and was dabbing her eyes.

'It's OK, son,' said Dad.

Archie suddenly felt a stab of indignation at how unfair it all was.

'What I don't understand,' he said, 'is why I got a dumb Fairy Demolition Contractor when if I'd known about this whole fairy thing, what I'd really have wanted, a million times more, is a Fairy Leg Surgeon for Mum.'

'Oh, love,' said Mum.

She blew her nose and looked at Archie.

'We're glad you got a Fairy Demolition Contractor,' she said.

Archie wasn't sure he'd heard her right. She said it again. Archie still didn't understand.

'Because,' said Mum, 'it's reminded me that there's something more important in life even than being able to walk.'

'Or having a job,' said Dad.

Archie still didn't understand.

'It's knowing that your son has a wonderful heart,' said Mum.

She beckoned Archie towards her, and just before her arms wrapped around him, he saw on her face something he hadn't seen there for a very long time.

A smile.

The hug lasted for ages, with Dad joining in. Mum cried some more. Soon all three of them were wet, and Archie noticed that Mum's mascara was making his school shirt look like a year-one art project.

Archie didn't mind.

He wouldn't have stopped her tears of happiness for anything, not even if he had a McDonald's bun.

Wipe Out

We're so anti-bacterial at our place.

Mum and Dad hate bacteria big time. Their main hobby is killing them.

I'm glad bacteria are just very tiny microbes the human eye can't see, because if they were any bigger we wouldn't be able to move at our place for the dead bodies.

'Callum,' Mum and Dad are always saying to me, 'wash your hands before dinner, then spray the bathroom. And after that, spray your bedroom, and your shoes, and the next-door's cat's bottom.'

We are the most anti-bacterial family I've ever met.

Here's what happens if you come to visit us.

You ring the doorbell by pressing a button that gets sprayed at least once a day with anti-bacterial bell-spraying fluid.

Mum answers the door using a handle that gets

wiped more than a bum. You follow her down the hall on a carpet Dad cleans with an anti-bacterial shampoo that me and my brother Troy aren't even allowed to touch in case it kills us and turns our fingernails green.

Dad's in the kitchen, wiping. Mum does some wiping too, then offers you a cup of tea. Don't have it, the cups taste of chemicals.

Why is Mum looking at you like that? She wants you to take your clothes off so she can run them through the machine using a laundry detergent that's soft, fragrant and very very anti-bacterial.

Get the picture?

Except it's not the whole picture. Because sometimes Mum doesn't want you to take your clothes off. Sometimes instead she clutches her tummy.

'Ow,' she says. Then she says it again, louder. 'Ow. Ow. Ow.'

Mum gets a lot of bad tummy pain.

Dad says it's not fair. We live in a house that's a death-zone for bacteria. In other parts of the world bacteria tell each other scary stories about our house. Yet Mum still gets terrible pain from tummy bugs.

I hate to see Mum in such pain. So do Dad and Troy. But we don't know what to do, so we just do more wiping.

Dad says it's a mystery, scientifically speaking.

I'm not a scientist, not yet. But I've been thinking

that maybe it isn't such a mystery.

Look at my friend Newt.

His house isn't anti-bacterial. I had tea at his place last week, and there was a lump of dried snot stuck to the dining table. OK, it might have been creamed spinach, but it definitely wasn't anti-bacterial.

His fridge has furry jam in it. So does his bathroom, on the taps.

His bedroom is like a sandstorm when you jump on the bed. It's mostly dandruff, but some of it's mouse poo from his pets, you can tell from the taste.

Newt's house must be the most bacterial place on the planet. But his mum never gets tummy pains, and nobody there gets headaches like Dad gets, and Newt doesn't have anxious dreams at night like me and Troy.

Ms Easton at school has just said something amazing.

She reckons some people are too anti-bacterial.

'Having a few of those bad bacteria around is good for us,' says Ms Easton, which sounds crazy but it's got to be right cause she's a teacher. 'They give our immune system something to practise on.'

'What's an immune system?' says Newt. 'Have I got one?'

Ms Easton gives him a look. She nods.

I think she's been to his house.

'We all have one,' she says. 'It's an important part of our body cells. The part that keeps us alive. Protects us against infection and disease.'

This is very interesting, scientifically speaking.

Specially to me.

'You said having a few of those bad bacteria is good,' I say to Ms Easton. 'How many's a few?'

'With those bad bacteria you don't want too many,' she says, glancing at Newt's hands. 'A billion. Two billion tops.'

That sounds like quite a lot to me.

Which is why I'm putting all the different bacteria things I can find into this health shake for Mum, so her immune system can get some practice at keeping her healthy.

I'm putting in old orange juice that's gone fizzy. Blue bits off some cheese I found in my camping bag. Milk that's had a fur ball from a cat soaking in it. Some stuff from under my fingernails. Some other stuff Newt kindly gave me.

There, all nicely blended.

I'll give it to Mum now before it curdles.

That didn't go very well. Dad says that what Mum just did, scientifically speaking, is called projectile vomiting.

'You said it was a heath shake,' wails Mum.

'It was,' I say. 'And it would have totally perked your immune system up big time, if you hadn't projectile-vomited it on Dad.'

'What's in it?' says Dad, peering suspiciously at his very messy shirt.

'Just some orange juice and cheese and other stuff,' I say. 'Stuff that's good for immune systems.'

'That's mouse poo,' says Troy, sniffing Dad's shirt. 'You can tell by the smell.'

I hate it when younger brothers try to be scientists.

'And what's this?' says Dad angrily. 'It looks like snot.'

'It could just be spinach,' I say. 'Or some other creamed leafy green vegetable with bacteria on it.'

But nobody hears me because Mum is clutching her stomach and moaning loudly. Her face is squished with pain.

Poor Mum, it's never been this bad.

I've got an awful feeling that part of it might be my fault.

We all hold her hand and stroke her arm and look anxious, and some of us say sympathetic things and some of us (me) say apologetic things, but it doesn't make her feel better.

Dad calls an ambulance.

The ambulance men gave me rude looks, and so did some of the other people here at the hospital. Cleaners mostly, because when they heard what I did, they sympathised with Mum and Dad. What Mum and Dad do for a hobby, they do for a living.

Dad has hardly spoken to me since we left the house.

I don't blame him. I'd be furious too if I had a son who'd poisoned his own mother.

I'm very worried about Mum. The emergency doctors and nurses took her away as soon as we arrived, straight after I confessed. We haven't seen her since, and that was hours ago.

One of the emergency doctors is coming back now.

Dad jumps up.

'How is she?' he says to the doctor.

Dad is pale with worry.

I know why. When Mum was a girl, she nearly died. Her immune system went seriously ga-ga and she had to spend weeks in hospital in an anti-bacterial ward.

People couldn't even bring her grapes.

Not even washed ones.

She got better in the end and was allowed to go home, but I think that's when she started wiping door knobs.

'She's asleep,' says the doctor to Dad. 'A couple of the tests we gave her required a minor anaesthetic.'

I can see Dad wants more information, but I get in first.

'Is she going to be OK?' I say. 'From the bacteria poisoning?'

The doctor looks at me.

I make a silent promise that if Mum gets through this, I'll be the most anti-bacterial person in our street. The germs won't stand a chance. Door knobs, carpets, next door's cat, I'll wipe and spray them all ten times a day. I'll stay home from school to do it. Ms Easton won't be able to stop me, not after her advice nearly killed my mum.

The doctor puts her hand on my shoulder.

I go very tense.

Can doctors arrest people for being badly informed and slightly too bacterial?

'You weren't totally off the beam, Callum,' the doctor says. 'If you'd given your mum the right kind of bacteria, it would have helped her, because some bacteria are good.'

I look at her, confused. I turn to Dad.

He's staring at the doctor, gobsmacked.

'Good bacteria?' he says.

We're both struggling with the idea.

'It's a bit complicated, scientifically speaking,' says the doctor. 'But basically there are good bacteria and there are bad bacteria. Your teacher was right, we need a few bad bacteria around so our immune systems don't get lazy. But to be really healthy we need billions of the good bacteria living inside us.'

That is amazing.

Wait till I tell Ms Easton.

Dad is open-mouthed, which I don't think is just so that good bacteria can find their way in.

'One of the tests we did on your wife,' says the doctor to Dad, 'involved putting a tiny camera inside her. It lets us see what's going on. What we saw was lots of swelling and inflammation. So we did some other tests which told us she's hardly got any good bacteria inside her at all.'

Dad doesn't say anything.

I can see what he's thinking.

Somebody has to say it.

'Is it cause our house is too anti-bacterial?' I ask the doctor.

The doctor frowns.

'Probably not,' she says. 'Your poor mum's got something that's called inflammatory digestive-tract disease. You can be born with it or you can just develop it, but it's always made worse by stress.'

'There's a lot of that in our house,' says Troy. 'Anti-bacterial stress.'

I love it when younger brothers back you up.

'Try not to worry,' says the doctor. 'We'll work out the right medicine for your mum and she shouldn't have the pains any more. And you can help by making her some yoghurt health shakes. Be sure to get the yoghurt with the good bacteria in it.'

I give Dad a nervous look.

I know he was planning to tell me that if I ever made Mum another health shake, he'd have me arrested.

Dad is frowning, which he does sometimes when he's thinking.

'Look at it this way,' the doctor says to him. 'What Callum did with the mouldy cheese and the mouse poo was a scientific experiment. Even when scientific experiments go wrong, they can still help us discover important things for the future.'

'I agree,' I say. 'And we've discovered something very important for Mum's future, bacterially speaking.'

Dad is staring at me, and he's still frowning.

But he's starting to look just a little bit proud.

We are so bacterial at our place.

We love bacteria big time. Our main hobby is making millions of yummy drinks with them. I'm glad bacteria are just tiny microbes, because if they were any bigger we wouldn't be able to fit them into our blender.

Or into our mum.

I told Ms Easton everything the doctor said, and she was very interested.

I told Newt too.

He was even more interested. He's planning to be a billionaire when he grows up, so he's always looking for business opportunities to get him started. He reckons this is a top opportunity.

He's invited kids from anti-bacterial homes round to his place to give their immune systems a workout.

He even put a sign in his front yard.

Germ Gym.

His mum made him take it down, but the anti-bacterial kids are still paying him two dollars a visit.

When I tell Mum, she laughs a lot and her tummy doesn't hurt even a tiny bit. She gives me a squeeze, and then she says something I'll never forget.

'I'm glad you don't want to be a billionaire,' she says. 'I'm glad you want to be a scientist. Because one day I reckon you'll do some experiments that won't just make one person's insides a better place, they'll make the whole world a better place.'

Dad and Troy are listening.

And nodding.

For a few moments I have inflammation of my whole body, but in a good way.

'Thanks,' I say.

Then we all sit down and watch TV, and we don't wipe the remote, not once.

Cumquat May

Walking to school, May wondered if she would be hit by a truck.

It didn't seem likely.

May was pretty sure trucks hardly ever came down Dumaresq Street, because of the speed bumps and the lollipop lady and the lack of truck-stop fuel and refreshment facilities.

So as usual she felt happy and safe. The sun was shining gently between the houses. The bamboo steamer she was hugging to her chest felt pleasantly warm inside its tea towel.

May wished Nan was here.

'See, Nan,' she'd say. 'Ancient Chinese wisdom isn't always right. We don't always have to be on guard against bad things. The lotus flower of happiness doesn't always have the slug of misery chomping away at it. And most days the truck of doom is miles away, stuck in a traffic jam.'

Actually she wouldn't say that. Nan got furious when she thought people were disrespecting ancient Chinese wisdom. And when Nan was furious, sometimes she used her knowledge of ancient Chinese swearwords.

May grinned.

Poor Nan.

She wished she could cheer Nan up with some traditional Australian wisdom. Dad was great at that. For a Chinese bloke his knowledge of traditional Australian wisdom was awesome.

'It's Friday,' Dad would probably say to Nan. 'Best day of the week, Friday. Thursday's over and the weekend's whistling at ya.'

If Nan scowled and started making a list of what could go wrong on a Friday, May would get in first.

'It's Friday and I've got two best friends and nine prawn-and-ginger dumplings,' she'd say. 'How good is that?'

With a carefree skip, May went in through the school gate. And discovered it wasn't as good as she'd thought.

Nowhere near as good.

At first, as May went across the playground, nothing seemed miserable or doomed at all.

Just a bit different.

She saw that somebody else was with April and June. A girl. The three of them were sitting in the

Calendar Club meeting place under the climbing frame. The place where April and May and June always had breakfast together.

May squinted, trying to see who it was.

The girl was a bit taller than April and June, and looked a bit older.

'Hi, May,' said April.

'Lo, May,' said June. 'This is Julie.'

'Julie's joining our club,' said April.

May felt shocked. And annoyed. Nobody had asked her.

'We had a vote,' said June. 'Me and April voted yes, so there wasn't any point waiting for you to vote, cause you'd be a majority.'

'Minority,' said Julie, looking May up and down.

'Julie's dad's got an amazing car,' said April. 'It's a Jugular.'

'Jaguar,' said Julie.

May didn't need to be told about the car. She recognised Julie now, the new girl who was repeating year six and who people said had been expelled from her last school.

Each morning her father dropped her off in the No Drop-Off Zone and then did a wheelie in the staff carpark.

'Hello,' said May quietly.

Julie didn't reply. Just stroked her very elegant hair which May calculated must have taken about a million hours to do. Unless going round corners very fast in a Jag made your hair get elegant by itself.

'So,' said Julie after a while, staring at May's tea-towel bundle. 'This must be the dumpling.'

There was something about the way Julie said it that didn't sound very friendly to May.

She saw June and April glance at each other nervously.

'Not dumpling,' said May to Julie. 'Dumplings. I've only got nine, which doesn't really divide into four. But you're the guest, so me and April and June will have two each and you can have three.'

May unwrapped the tea towel.

Julie looked the steamer up and down.

May was shocked to see she was doing it with what looked like a sneer. Nobody sneered at Nan's dumplings. They were famous throughout the district. Well, maybe not the whole district, but they were famous throughout the Calendar Club.

'We're having organic sourdough toast,' said Julie.

She stood up and pulled a toaster out of the most expensive-looking school bag May had ever seen. It was also the most expensive-looking toaster May had ever seen. Gleaming. Elegant. Not a crumb on it.

'Where can I plug this in?' said Julie to April and June.

April and June scrambled to their feet.

'Over there,' said April, pointing to the porch outside the library.

'It's where the teachers plug the loudspeaker

system in for jazz dodgeball,' said June. 'I'll show you.'

May wrapped the steamer back up to keep the dumplings warm.

Dumplings and toast. Quite nice actually. She'd often had it.

She watched June and April setting off towards the library porch with Julie and reminded herself of another piece of Dad's traditional Australian wisdom.

You're a mug if you don't give people a second chance.

Julie was probably just nervous about being in a new school and anxious about making friends.

After a few steps, Julie stopped and turned back to May, holding out some very expensive-looking bread.

That's nice of her, thought May. She's going to ask how I like my toast.

'I've only got nine slices,' said Julie. 'Not enough for you. But you've got dumplings. Enjoy your dumplings, dumpling.'

She headed off to plug in her toaster.

May stared.

What did she just say?

April and June were looking shocked too.

The year before, when May had started at the school, the head teacher had taken her aside.

'We're a friendly and very inclusive school community, May,' she'd said. 'So I don't expect you to have any trouble. But if anybody does call you a name, you must tell me, OK?'

May had been puzzled.

'What sort of name?' she said.

The head teacher looked uncomfortable.

'Oh, I don't know,' she said. 'Dumpling, for example. Something like that.'

May was still puzzled.

'My mum and dad call me dumpling all the time,' she said.

The head teacher looked more uncomfortable.

'Yes,' she said, 'but if someone calls you that here, it'll be different. They'll be trying to hurt your feelings. On account of where your family comes from and you being a bit plump. If anyone calls you dumpling here, I need to know, OK?'

Nobody had. Not the whole year.

Until now.

May glared at Julie, who was crouching by the jazz dodgeball socket.

That was your second chance, thought May. I'm starting to think you're not just an anxious new girl, I'm starting to think you're also an extremely rude person.

She waited for April and June to give rude Julie the flick and come back over to the climbing frame and have their Calendar Club breakfast as usual.

So far they weren't moving.

Julie turned from the jazz dodgeball socket and called to them.

'Toast'll be ready soon,' she said. 'You'll love this marmalade. It's from Paris.'

May snorted.

This new kid didn't have a clue. If she thought a bit of organic toast and Paris marmalade was going to break up the Calendar Club, she was dreaming.

Except April and June still weren't coming back.

They were looking at May guiltily.

April was giving her a shrug.

May felt a chill wind touch her deep inside. The sort of wind you feel when a truck's brakes have failed in the distance and the truck is hurtling towards you.

It wasn't actually a truck, but when April and June walked away from her and over to Julie, it felt like one.

May sat under the climbing frame, miserably chewing a dumpling.

She felt numb.

How could they do it? Invite an outsider to join the Calendar Club? A rude pushy outsider who didn't even like dumplings. And who didn't even have the right name.

May had always known that April and June were hopeless at spelling, but April, May, June, Julie? That was ridiculous.

The things people do, thought May, for the chance of a ride in a Jag and the hope of non-frizzy hair.

Pathetic.

'Nice dumplings,' said a voice.

May looked up.

A boy was grinning down at her from the top of the climbing frame. May recognised him from one of the other year-six classes. She didn't know his name and she didn't particularly want to, not at the moment.

'We have dumplings too where I come from,' said the boy. 'They're called Mantu. Those look good.'

May remembered that the boy was from Afghanistan.

'What's in those?' he said.

May could see he was hoping she'd offer him one.

She was tempted to say prawn toenails and pigs' bumholes to get him to leave, but she didn't. They might be delicacies in Afghanistan.

'Do you mind?' she said. 'I've got important things to think about.'

'Sorry,' said the boy.

He was still looking at the dumplings and his dark eyes were so wistful that May suddenly grabbed a dumpling and held it up to him.

'Thanks,' he said, taking it. 'My name's Karim.'

May realised to her horror that he was climbing down towards her, probably to sit next to her.

That's all she needed. Word getting around that poor pathetic Dumpling May was so desperate for a friend, she was hanging out with a boy.

'I'm very busy,' she said.

The boy's face clouded.

'OK,' he said quietly. 'Thanks for the dumpling.'

As he headed off across the playground through the yelling kids, May felt a twinge of guilt. She pushed it away.

She'd been telling the truth. She was very busy. Waiting for her best friends to come to their senses. To remember who their real friend was. To spot the difference between a real friend and a pig's bum-hole.

'Nan,' yelled May, rushing into the kitchen. 'I need dumplings.'

Nan came in from the backyard with the scrap bucket, frowning and deep in thought.

'The chooks have stopped laying,' she said. 'I think it's global warming.'

May sighed.

'They haven't stopped laying, Nan,' she said. 'I collected the eggs before school.'

Nan took this in and looked at May sternly.

'We've talked about this, Mabel,' she said. 'I don't want you getting up so early. You must sleep in as late as you can on school mornings. Knowledge seeks a rested mind.'

May resisted the temptation to argue. Or to remind Nan how much she hated being called Mabel. This was more urgent.

'I need your help, Nan,' she said. 'I need you to help me make some very good dumplings.'

'What about the ones we made yesterday?' said Nan. Her eyes widened with alarm. 'Did they get stolen? I told you to watch out for thieves on the way to school.'

'Trucks, Nan,' said May wearily. 'You told me to watch out for trucks.'

'Those as well,' said Nan. 'Why do you need more dumplings now?

May told Nan about Julie and the toast and the Jaguar and the Paris marmalade.

She told her about all the times during the day she'd thought April and June would come to their senses.

And how they hadn't.

Nan put her arms round May and hugged her for a long time.

'I understand now,' she said softly. 'You want special dumplings.'

May felt relief seep through her like the broth in freshly steamed Xiao Long Bao, which when Nan made them were dumpling magic.

'You want dumplings so special,' said Nan, 'so delicious, so tantalising, so irresistible, that all who smell them will fall under their power and no toasted breakfast treat in the world will stand a chance of stealing your friends away.'

May felt tears of gratitude filling her eyes.

Sometimes ancient Chinese wisdom was a wonderful thing.

'You want superdumplings,' murmured Nan.

'Megadumplings. Dumplings that will blow July out of the water.'

'Her name's Julie,' said May. 'But apart from that you're spot on.'

Nan gave a long sigh.

May felt a stab of anxiety. She'd heard that sigh many times before. The relief started to trickle out of her like the broth in a Xiao Long Bao that some idiot has tried to pick up with a fork.

'Oh Mabel, Mabel, Mabel, Mabel,' said Nan. 'Dumplings aren't weapons of war. And even if they were, no friendship has ever been won with a weapon of war. Trying to win friendship with a weapon of war is like trying to pick up water with chopsticks.'

May gave a despairing groan.

For Nan, everything in the world that she didn't agree with was like trying to pick up water with chopsticks.

'Please,' said May. 'I'm desperate.'

Nan grabbed a pair of chopsticks and reached over to the sink and tried to pick up water with them.

May gave another groan.

Nan gave her another hug.

'If a friendship is a friendship,' said Nan, 'it will be a friendship. Now help me get dinner. We're having fish fingers.'

May slumped back in her chair.

It was hopeless.

She'd never hated ancient Chinese wisdom as much as she did now.

Faintly, through her despair, May heard the distant sound of Dad's voice in her memory. The advice he'd given her the day she'd left to come to the city to live.

'Pay attention to the wisdom of others,' he'd said, 'but listen even more carefully to your own heart.'

She'd almost forgotten that.

Now she was glad she hadn't. Because he was totally right.

'Thanks, Dad,' she whispered.

May sat on her bed, deep in thought.

A new club. That's what she needed. A new Calendar Club with really good friends in it. Friends who wouldn't dump her the first time French marmalade came along.

Trouble was, there were only three girls in the whole school with Calendar Club names.

April, May and June.

May stared at the wall, desperate.

So desperate that for a few crazy moments she seriously considered letting boys join the Calendar Club. And making them only use the first few letters of their names.

Augie.

Septimus.

Declan.

Maybe one of them would even have a pet called Octopus.

For a brief moment it all seemed possible. Until she remembered she didn't know any boys called Augie, Septimus or Declan. And even if she found some, they were boys, so what would she talk to them about? Plus she was pretty sure boys liked marmalade even more than girls did.

No, it would have to be dumplings. And if Nan wouldn't help her, she'd make them herself.

They would be the most amazing dumplings anyone had ever seen. Dumplings that April and June wouldn't be able to resist. Dumplings that would have them begging to be let back into the Calendar Club.

Strawberry dumplings.

Chocolate dumplings.

Marmalade dumplings.

May grabbed her school bag to find a pen to make a list. There was usually one somewhere in the bottom of the bag. It just took a bit of rummaging.

She rummaged. And felt something.

It wasn't a pen, it was a small piece of paper, folded tight.

She unfolded it. A note.

Dear May,
Sorry we broke up the club, but we got sick
of dumplings. Totally sick. We're over them.
We never want to eat another dumpling in
our whole life.
Sorry.
April and June.

May stared at the note for a long time.

She thought about Mum and Dad and how happy they'd be if she went back to live with them on the farm. And did school on the computer like before and told them she didn't mind living hundreds of kilometres from civilisation and never seeing another kid in actual person.

Happy, but they would know it wasn't really true.

'May,' Dad would say gently. 'Friendship's not a hobby, it's a job. And you don't get to knock off early on Fridays.'

'Life isn't meant to be easy,' Mum would say, because she was an expert at traditional Australian wisdom too. 'Fun, but not easy.'

May felt tears stinging her eyes.

Mum and Dad wanted the best for her, she knew that. They loved her so much they were prepared to only see her during school holidays, so she could have the best. A real school. And real friends.

They'd be really sad if they knew how lonely she felt right now. And really disappointed.

May heard a sloshing sound coming from the backyard.

She knew what it was, but to take her mind off Mum and Dad, she peered out the window.

Nan was doing what she did every night. Tipping the washing-up water onto the roots of her cumquat tree. Well, Nan called it washing-up water, but it wasn't the ordinary sort. For a start it had veggie water in it, plus the water Nan soaked her fermented bean curd in. And floating in it were leftover bits of the dried Chinese herbs and twigs Nan boiled up to make ancient potions that cured flu and kept cutlery shiny.

'Very good for the cumquats, this water,' Nan often said. 'Look at them. Supercumquats. Megacumquats.'

May looked at the cumquats now, small orange fruit glowing against dark green leaves in the light from the kitchen.

They didn't look particularly super. Or mega. They never did. Just like small oranges really.

But May knew they were different. And quite unusual. She hadn't heard of a single other garden in the whole district that had a cumquat tree.

Perhaps, thought May, it's not the size that makes them super and mega. Perhaps it's their flavour.

Except the flavour of cumquats was bitter.

Which was why people made marmalade from them.

'Mabel, what are you doing? This is not sleeping. Knowledge will not seek a mind that is banging around in the kitchen at three o'clock in the morning.'

Nan stood in the doorway, glaring.

May sighed.

She'd tried to be as quiet as she could, but obviously she hadn't been quiet enough.

Nan was staring at the pile of cumquats on the kitchen table. All washed and some of them cut into pieces.

'What are you doing?' said Nan again.

May suddenly wished she'd talked to Nan about this before she'd started. Got her permission to pick the cumquats.

'I'm making marmalade,' said May quietly.

She knew exactly what Nan would say next. A cumquat picked sneakily in the dead of night is an unhappy cumquat. Marmalade isn't a weapon of war. Things like that.

'Marmalade,' said Nan, 'isn't a victim of war.'

May looked at Nan.

That wasn't what she'd expected, and she wasn't exactly sure what it meant.

'Those cumquats you've cut up,' said Nan. 'They look like they've been stabbed and shot. To make marmalade you need to slice the fruit very thin. And where are the pips?'

'I threw them out,' said May.

'You need the pips,' said Nan. 'The pips make the marmalade set. Don't throw any more out. And cut the fruit thin. Here, let me show you.'

Nan rolled up the sleeves of her nightie and started slicing a cumquat.

May watched, feeling a bit dazed and not just because it was three in the morning.

'Nan,' she said after a while. 'You know why I'm making this marmalade, don't you?'

Nan nodded. She handed May the knife. 'Now you do it.'

May started carefully slicing.

'So you don't think,' she said to Nan, 'that making this marmalade to win my friends back is like trying to pick up water with chopsticks?'

Nan shook her head.

May sliced silently, a bit confused. After a while she looked at Nan again.

'Why did you change your mind?' she said.

Nan gave her a little smile.

'Modern Chinese wisdom,' she said.

Walking to school on Monday, May felt like she'd been hit by a truck.

Well, her arms did.

She'd never chopped anything for so long.

But it was worth it. As she walked, she could hear the jars of cumquat marmalade clinking gently in her school bag.

May smiled, even though her insides were prickling with anxiety.

If this didn't work, she'd still be grateful that Nan had discovered modern Chinese wisdom.

But she hoped it would work. Which was why she'd set out earlier than usual. To make sure her toaster, the one Nan had pulled out from under the house and dusted off for her, was set up and plugged in before Julie arrived.

It felt good, arriving at school this early.

With a hopeful skip, May went in through the school gate.

And discovered she wasn't early enough.

Julie was over by the jazz dodgeball socket, behind a very large folding table.

Hundreds of paper plates were laid out on the table. And tubs of butter. And bags of bread. And jars of marmalade.

Good grief, thought May. She's making toast for the whole school. She must want friends even more badly than me.

April and June were with Julie, crouching over several toasters.

May felt like giving up. Turning round and going home. Telling Nan she felt ill, which was true.

But the thought of doing that made her feel even worse.

What a sad waste of so much hard work and cumquat marmalade and modern Chinese wisdom.

Instead, May stood behind a tree and waited.

After a while, Julie went into the girls' toilet.

She's probably feeling nervous, thought May. With so much at stake. Or else she's got a few cappuccino machines plugged in there.

May, feeling quite nervous herself, went over to April and June. They looked startled when they saw her.

'You shouldn't be here,' said April. 'This is embarrassing.'

'I just wanted to give you these,' said May.

She took the jars of cumquat marmalade out of her bag and put them on the table.

April and June stared at them.

'Julie's already got marmalade,' said June. 'From that France place. This is really embarrassing.'

'Taste it,' said May.

April and June looked doubtful.

May took the lid off a jar and held it out to April.

April glanced around nervously to check that Julie was still in the toilets. Then she stuck a tiny part of the tip of one finger into the cumquat marmalade and tasted it.

Her eyes widened.

She tasted some more.

June tasted some too. Her eyes widened as well.

'These jars are for you,' said May to April and June. 'But if you want to use them this morning, that's fine with me.'

She walked away, back to the tree.

After a while, Julie returned to the table.

May watched as April and June showed her the jars of cumquat marmalade. They didn't point to the tree, so it didn't look like they were telling Julie who the marmalade came from.

Julie was frowning, annoyed, probably because she could see this new marmalade didn't come from Paris. But there wasn't time to do anything about it.

Kids were arriving at school. Coming over to the table, curious. Helping themselves to toast.

More and more of them, arriving in groups.

April, June and Julie were suddenly frantic with the toasters, keeping up the supply.

Kids were buttering their own toast. And, May saw, smearing on their own marmalade. Some chose Paris, some cumquat.

May forced herself to keep breathing as she watched. Her insides were aching.

There was a swarm around the table now and the toast-makers were barely keeping up. The playground was buzzing.

Still more kids were arriving.

And teachers.

For a moment it looked like the teachers were going to stop the whole thing, until one of them nibbled a slice of toast that a student handed her and then stared at it, amazed.

May guessed it had cumquat marmalade on it.

Gradually, she saw, the crowd was realising that the two marmalades were very different. People were grabbing jars of cumquat marmalade and sticking their fingers in and having another taste.

Telling their friends to taste it too.

May couldn't hear what was being said in the hubbub, but she could see lots of kids talking to Julie with excited hand movements that looked grateful and very enthusiastic.

Julie, glowing, was responding with the sort of hand movements people use when they're boasting that their marmalade comes from Paris.

May knew this was the moment.

The moment to go over and tell everyone the truth. Tell them who they should be thanking for the marmalade. And then it would be her that everyone would be excitedly crowding around, desperate to be her friend, begging her to bring cumquat marmalade every morning.

And she could. There were thirty-seven more jars of it at home.

She'd be Cumquat May, the leader of the Cumquat Club, the most popular girl in the whole school.

It was a wonderful thought, and May was tempted.

Very tempted.

She took a step forward.

Then stopped.

She thought about Nan. About friendship and weapons of war. She thought about Dad too. About listening carefully to your own heart.

May felt lucky to have so much wisdom in her life. And so much love.

Perhaps though, she thought, it's time I started working out some wisdom of my own.

The thought glowed inside her, warm as the filling in a just-made dumpling.

May stood there a while longer.

Then she gave one last look at the clamouring mob of excited marmalade fans, turned, and walked slowly away across the playground.

When she was halfway across, she saw that over on the other side a solitary figure was sitting against the fence, eating from a plastic lunchbox.

As she got closer, he looked up and gave her a friendly grin.

It was Karim.

May smiled back, went over and sat down next to him.

He offered her his lunchbox.

She took it.

'Nice dumplings,' she said.

The Tortoise
And The Hair

Vic didn't slow down when he reached the pet
shop.

'Mind your backs,' he called out as he sprinted
straight inside. 'Urgent delivery coming through.'

Vic knew kids weren't meant to run in shops,
and he knew at this speed there was a danger of
tripping over a kennel and ending up nose-first in
a sack of pigs' ears. But he had to take the risk. He
was seriously late.

Nothing must slow him down.

Please don't stutter, thought Vic as he thudded
into the counter. Please don't stutter, please don't
stutter, please don't stutter.

Behind the counter, Mr Pappadopoulis looked
up, frowned at Vic and began to stutter.

'H – h – h – h – h – h – h – h – h –'

No, thought Vic. Please. I haven't got time for
this.

'H – h – h – h – h – h – h – h –'

Vic knew what Mr Pappadopoulis was trying to say.

'Hello,' said Vic, getting in first to save Mr Pappadopoulis the trouble and more importantly to save time.

'W – w – w – w – w – w – w – w – w –'

Please, begged Vic silently. Let me do the talking.

Mr Pappadopoulis didn't.

'W – w – w – w – w – w – w – w – w –'

Once again, Vic guessed what Mr Pappadopoulis was trying to say.

'What,' said Vic, 'can you do for me? Thanks for asking.'

He reached into his sports bag and took out Monty.

'Gran's tortoise needs a clip,' he said.

Mr Pappadopoulis peered at Monty and frowned again.

'T – t – t – t – t – t – t –' he said. 'T – t – t – t – t –'

'Toenails, that's right,' said Vic. 'Gran's hoping you can do it. Her hands shake too much and the last time I tried, I accidently dropped Monty into a laundry bucket full of starch.'

Monty blinked.

So did Mr Pappadopoulis.

'I know,' said Vic. 'Poor Monty. The last thing a tortoise needs is to end up stiffer and even slower. But I was in a rush and I slipped.'

'S – s – s – s – s – s – s –' said Mr Pappadopoulis.

Vic was puzzled for a moment, then got it.

'Sling him over to you? Thanks, Mr P,' said Vic, handing Monty to Mr Pappadopoulis. 'Sorry I can't stay to chat, I'm in the school athletics team and I'm late for the District Championships. My phone number's on Monty's tummy. Bye.'

As Vic sprinted out of the shop, he glimpsed puppies, fish, guinea pigs and terrapins all looking at him disapprovingly.

That was a bit unkind, the pets' faces said. *Don't you know anything about stuttering? Don't you know that rushing a stutterer is the worst thing you can do?*

Vic pushed the guilt away and sprinted down the street. Those puppies and fish and guinea pigs and terrapins obviously didn't know anything about being in a district championship relay team.

Vic glanced at his watch.

Twenty-eight minutes till the team bus left.

Enough time.

Probably.

The tortoise was done, only the hair to go.

Please don't gossip, thought Vic as he rushed into Uncle Riad's hair salon. Please don't gossip, please don't gossip, please don't gossip.

Uncle Riad was with a customer, blow-drying a cascade of Beyoncé curls. He looked up, saw Vic and gave him a grin.

'How's the champ?' he said. 'I was just telling

Leonie here what a killer you are on the track. How you're gunna blow the opposition away today. Wipe the track with 'em. Bring home a fistful of trophies. Even better, those engraved silver carving platters.'

'I'm only in the relay team,' muttered Vic.

'Vic runs the final legs of all the relays,' said Uncle Riad to Leonie. 'The four times one hundred metres, the four times two hundred metres and, wait for it, the four times four hundred metres. Creams 'em every time.'

Leonie looked impressed.

'Thanks, Uncle Riad,' said Vic. 'But I'm in a bit of a hurry.' He took Gran's wig from his sports bag and held it out. 'Gran says it needs a trim.'

Uncle Riad didn't even look at the wig, just kept on gossiping to Leonie.

'You'd never have guessed,' said Uncle Riad, 'if you'd seen his wobbly thighs when he was little. He didn't walk till he was two and a half.'

Vic wondered if Uncle Riad had heard any part of 'needs a trim' and 'bit of a hurry'. Maybe Uncle Riad had a build-up of hair clippings in his ears.

'Vic's parents would be so proud if they could see him now,' Uncle Riad was saying to Leonie. 'Be a winner, that's what they always told him. That's why they called him Victor.'

Take the wig, begged Vic silently. Please take it.

'Throw yourself at life,' said Uncle Riad, looking fondly at Vic. 'That's what his dad always said. Go full pelt. Do whatever it takes to get in front of the other mongrels.'

Take it, pleaded Vic. Take it, take it, take it.

'If only his parents were still here to see what a champ their son has turned into,' said Uncle Riad. He sighed. 'If only they hadn't driven quite so fast. Through that red light.'

Vic glanced at his watch.

Thirteen minutes till the bus left.

He stuffed the wig into Uncle Riad's hands. Uncle Riad stared at it, frowning.

'What happened?' he said.

'Got a bit melted in the toaster,' said Vic. 'I was in a hurry, making Gran's toast and trimming her split ends at the same time. Bye.'

He turned and sprinted out of the salon.

The sounds of the hair dryer and Uncle Riad's voice drifted after him.

'Blow 'em away, champ.'

Please don't be gone, thought Vic as he ran towards the school gate. Please don't be gone, please don't be gone, please don't be gone.

If the bus was gone, so was his place in the team. Mr Callaghan the sports teacher was fanatical about being on time. He didn't like lateness at the finishing line, or anywhere.

Vic's chest was hurting with effort and stress.

Thirteen minutes from Uncle Riad's salon should have been plenty, he thought bitterly. It would have, if the streets hadn't been jammed with dawdlers and slowcoaches.

Old people who needed to peer into every shop window, probably looking for a product that would get starch out of their pants.

Gangs of teenagers meandering along, gawking at their phones, probably checking the *Guinness Book of Records* website to see if they'd broken the record for the slowest dawdle through a shopping centre.

Families pausing all over the footpath to taste each other's ice-creams.

Vic had very nearly crashed into a mum and dad and kids with chocolate and pistachio moustaches, and he'd felt a bit jealous. Then, as he'd pushed past them, a bit sticky.

Please don't be gone, begged Vic again.

He sprinted through the school gate and round the corner of the library to the staff carpark.

There it was. The team bus.

He'd made it.

'Victor,' said a voice. 'What are you doing here?'

Vic stopped and turned round.

Mr Downie the principal was coming out of the library.

'Didn't you get our message?' said Mr Downie.

Vic looked at him, confused.

'We sent you a text last night,' said Mr Downie. 'You're not running today. Sorry.'

Vic stared.

Not running?

'I discussed it with Mr Callaghan,' said Mr Downie. 'We agreed you haven't been putting in your best times lately and you could do with a rest. Didn't you look at your phone?'

Vic was so dazed he could hardly think.

He had to admit he probably hadn't looked at his phone last night, what with his evening training programme and cooking Gran's tea and Uncle Riad coming round and challenging him to an arm wrestle.

'Have the weekend off, Victor,' said Mr Downie. 'Do something relaxing. Take it easy.'

The principal went back into the library.

Vic slumped against the wall. It was true, his times had dropped lately. But he'd hoped it was just temporary while he was saving up for new running shoes. Which had taken longer than he'd planned because he hadn't wanted to put extra financial pressure on Gran. It was hard enough for her, with all the debts Mum and Dad had left.

The strange thing, though, was that even when Uncle Riad had found out he needed new running shoes and bought him a pair, plus a luminous green singlet that said *Champ*, his times hadn't picked up.

That was very strange.

And worrying.

Vic stared numbly across the carpark.

Mr Callaghan was getting onto the bus. He gave

Vic an embarrassed wave. The bus door closed behind him. Vic could see the faces of the athletics team silhouetted in the windows.

The bus started to drive away.

Vic heard a voice inside his head.

'Be a winner,' said the voice. 'Because if you're not a winner, you're a loser.'

He wasn't sure if it was his dad's voice, or Uncle Riad's, or Donald Trump's.

Vic didn't care.

He gripped his sports bag and ran after the bus.

By the time Vic caught up with the bus, it was going quite fast.

It had started slowly, turning a few corners, but now it was on a long straight downhill street and was already in third gear.

Vic was running the race of his life.

He'd stopped feeling the pain in his legs several hundred metres back. All he could feel now was a searing fire in his chest and the blood pounding in his head and his eardrums about to explode.

And lower down, in his guts, sadness.

Which he wasn't surprised by.

He'd been dumped. Dumped by the team he'd done so much for. Including giving up ice-cream because of the risk of flab.

Vic was tempted to stop running and give the sticky patch of chocolate and pistachio on his shoulder a good lick and just enjoy it.

But he didn't.

He forced a last spurt of effort into his legs, ignored the agony in his lungs, caught up with the bus and pounded on the back window.

In the driver's-side rear-vision mirror he saw the driver's face go wide-eyed with shock, and Vic remembered just in time to drop back as the driver hit the brakes.

As Vic staggered up the steps onto the bus, he saw it wasn't just the driver who was in shock.

Mr Callaghan and all the kids were staring at him too. Mouths almost as wide as his, and he was the one gasping for air.

As soon as Vic saw Mr Callaghan's face, he knew he was going to get his place in the team back. And he did. Mr Callaghan started giving it to him even before the bus door was closed.

'That was amazing, young man. An amazing piece of running. In the light of such an improved performance . . .'

Vic tried to let Mr Callaghan know that he needed to sit down.

He couldn't speak for the moment, so he let Mr Callaghan know by getting very dizzy and dropping his bag and almost fainting.

Mr Callaghan jumped up and lowered Vic into his seat.

'Head between your legs,' said Mr Callaghan. 'Get some blood back to your brain.'

Vic leaned forward and lowered his head.

He found himself looking at his bag on the floor between his feet. It was half open and he could see his phone.

There was a message on the screen from Mr Pappadopoulis.

The bus was moving again now and Vic was still a bit dizzy, so the words in the message were blurry and hard to make out.

Monty must be finished, thought Vic. Trimmed and ready to be picked up. Gee, that was quick.

He blinked a few times and suddenly he could read the message clearly.

Have you thought of slowing down?
Winning isn't the only thing in life.
Take time to decide what's important to you.
Silly boy.

Vic stared at the message. There was something about the first letter of each sentence . . .

Then he remembered what Mr Pappadopoulis had stammered in the pet shop.

H – h – h – h – h –

W – w – w – w – w –

T – t – t – t – t –

S – s – s – s – s –

Vic had thought in the shop he'd known what Mr Pappadopoulis was trying to say, but he hadn't.

He did now.

It was here, in the message.

Vic read the message again. And again.

He kept on reading it until Mr Callaghan started booming in his ear.

'How are you feeling, lad? Back to your senses?'

'Yes, Mr Callaghan,' said Vic quietly. 'I am.'

'Good to hear,' said Mr Callaghan. 'Because in the light of your performance today, you're back in the team.'

Vic looked around the bus. All the kids were nodding. Except one.

Garth Watson.

Garth must be his replacement.

'What about Garth?' said Vic to Mr Callaghan.

'Garth won't mind stepping down,' said Mr Callaghan. 'In the circumstances.'

Vic could see that Garth did mind.

A lot.

Vic zipped up his sports bag.

'Thanks for the offer,' he said to Mr Callaghan. 'But I've decided not to be in the team any more.'

Mr Callaghan stared at him.

'Can I get off the bus please?' said Vic.

'No,' said Mr Callaghan. 'You can't.'

Vic could see from Mr Callaghan's face that Mr Callaghan was going to try to make him stay in the team. Vic didn't want to have to sit through that. He had more important things to do.

He stood up and smashed the emergency glass panel with his phone and pulled the emergency lever.

An alarm went off and the driver swore loudly

and pulled over to the side of the road. The bus door opened with a hiss. Even as the driver was turning round to see what the trouble was, Vic was stepping past him and out the door.

'Sorry about the glass panel,' said Vic.

'Make sure you haven't left anything on the bus,' muttered the driver.

Vic didn't reply.

He had left some things on the bus. Not his sports bag or phone. A couple of things he didn't need any more.

Years later he would tell his own kids how much better his life had been after he'd left those things on the bus. After he'd left behind the dopey idea that if you run fast enough, you can get away from sadness. And after he'd ditched the desperate hope that if you run even faster, you can catch up with what you've lost and get it back.

Get them back.

Vic walked slowly away from the bus.

He ignored Mr Callaghan's angry shouts, which stopped eventually when the bus engine started up again.

There was no hurry.

Vic had the whole day ahead of him. With not a lot planned.

He fancied some quiet time with Gran. Washing her wig, with a bit of conditioner to add bounce and vitality.

Then a stroll with Monty, who'd probably be

keen to check out the back garden now his toenails were in working order.

And this evening, a couple of hours on his own with Gran's family photo album.

Just taking it slowly.

But first, a cup of tea with Mr Pappadopoulis. And a relaxed chat.

It didn't have to be a long one.

Vic didn't need to say much. He didn't need to say please don't stutter or please don't gossip or please don't be gone.

Just two words.

Thank you.

Chips That Pass In The Night

When I ask for fifty dollars worth of chips, the man behind the counter in the fish and chip shop gives me a funny look.

'No salt, thanks,' I say.

Ernie isn't meant to eat salt. He's not meant to eat chips either, but they won't kill him. They won't be able to. Something else is doing that.

'Fifty dollars?' says the man. 'Are you sure?'

He's looking at me very suspiciously. I don't know why. There's no law against kids buying chips.

I'm tempted to tell him about Ernie. How much Ernie loves chips. How Ernie has said more than once that in his opinion, chips are magic.

I decide not to say anything in case he thinks Ernie is a silly old man.

Instead I show him my fifty-dollar note. It's the first fifty-dollar note I've ever had. I wait to see if it works like I always imagined it would.

It does.

The fish and chip man grunts and shovels chips into a big wire basket.

I hope this won't take long. If anyone sees me here, such as Mum or Dad or Uncle Mal or Auntie Liz, I'm history. And poor Ernie will die disappointed.

'Bags or box?' says the fish and chip man.

'Can you wrap them in newspaper?' I ask.

I think Ernie will enjoy them more that way. They might remind him of his childhood. When he was happy. Before everything happened.

'We don't do newspaper,' says the man.

I don't believe him. He looks almost as old as Ernie. He's got nose hairs, plus elastic straps over his shirt holding up his very baggy trousers. I don't think he's modern enough to get his news online.

A woman who's battering fish behind the counter glares at him.

'Stop being a grump,' she says. 'There's some in the kitchen.'

She must be the man's wife because he doesn't start an argument, just rolls his eyes and goes out the back.

'Thanks,' I say to the woman.

The woman gives me a look.

'Your mum needs to do some cooking classes, young man,' she says.

Which is a cheek because she doesn't even know Mum.

I'm tempted to tell her that Mum doesn't need to cook because she's got all Ernie's money and she and Dad can afford home delivery every night.

But I don't. It's bad enough that Ernie is poor and sick, without all his personal financial details being made public in a fish and chip shop.

A girl is standing near the shop.

'Do you want a chip?' she says.

She's holding out a small bag of them.

It's nice of her, offering one to a complete stranger. But a bit surprising. Can't she see I've just come out of the same shop that she must have been in? And that I'm holding a huge parcel that smells very strongly of exactly what she's offering.

'No thanks,' I say.

The girl's shoulders sag.

She looks so disappointed I'm tempted to take one. But my parcel is heavy and droopy and I need both hands to hold it.

Plus I've got to get these chips to Ernie before it's too late.

'Why doesn't anyone want one?' mutters the girl.

She doesn't look disappointed any more, just angry. Which makes me feel nervous. She's about my age, but bigger and I'm pretty sure she'd be stronger.

My life savings are invested in these chips. If she starts any rough stuff, this newspaper could easily split open.

'Sorry,' I say. 'I would have one of your chips normally. Probably a few. But I've already got some and I'm in a hurry. Thanks anyway. Bye.'

I walk away.

After a couple of moments I realise the girl is walking next to me, staring at my parcel.

'You must have a seriously big family,' she says. 'And pets that like chips.'

She doesn't sound angry now, just sort of wistful.

'These aren't for my family,' I say. 'They're for someone else.'

The girl frowns as if she doesn't believe me.

She might have a point. Ernie is Mum's ex-husband, so in a way we're related. Even though he and Mum got divorced before Mum and Dad had me.

'You're right,' I say. 'Ernie is sort of my family. Well, he feels like he is.'

Why am I telling her all this?

'Why are you giving him so many chips?' says the girl.

She's very nosy for a complete stranger. But there's something about the way she's looking at me. Like she really wants to know.

I blurt it out.

'People have been very mean to Ernie,' I say. 'And now he's very sick. Before he dies I want him to see that at least one person really likes him.'

Now that I've said it out loud, it sounds sort of dumb.

If Mum and Dad heard me say it, that's the word they'd use. Dumb. And stupid. And feeble-brained.

The girl gives a soft whistle. She doesn't sound like she thinks it's dumb.

'You must really like him,' she says. 'To give him that many chips.'

I look at her. For a person who's a complete stranger she's extremely understanding.

I want to ask her why she was giving away chips. And why she was so disappointed and angry that people wouldn't take them. But I don't know how to put the question into words. I'm not very good at asking girls personal things.

All I can think of is what Mum and Dad would say if they were here.

'That's not how the world works, Jackson,' they'd say. 'Only imbeciles and con artists give things away. Ditch that little twerp now.'

I hope the girl can't tell from my face what I'm thinking.

Probably not. She isn't looking hurt or cross. She's staring at the ground, her hands in her coat pockets, frowning thoughtfully.

Then suddenly, as if by magic, the words come out of my mouth.

'Why were you doing that?' I say. 'Being so generous with your chips?'

The girl looks at me for a few moments. As if she's not sure whether to answer me.

'I'm trying to learn a hard thing,' she says softly.

'What?' I say.

'To forgive potatoes,' she says.

I try not to stare at her. From the tone of her voice I can tell it isn't a joke. It sounds like it's something very important to her. I try not to let her see that I haven't got a clue what she's talking about.

This always happens when I talk to girls, me ending up feeling awkward and embarrassed.

The girl is looking like she doesn't know what to say now either. She's staring at the ground again.

Suddenly I'm feeling even more awkward and embarrassed at the idea that she might be feeling awkward and embarrassed. I wish we could just say goodbye and leave it at that.

It'll have to be me who says it, to get both of us out of this.

I rehearse it in my mind.

'Very nice meeting you. I have to go now. Bye.'

I try to say it.

I can't.

The girl turns to me.

'Can I come with you?' she says. 'To see Ernie?'

As we head towards the hospital, I hope I'm not doing the wrong thing.

What if Ernie doesn't want a stranger seeing what's happened to him and where his life has ended up?

And what if I get even more embarrassed and

stressed from being with this girl and I have to be hospitalised?

In a different ward to Ernie?

'What sort of very mean?' says the girl.

I look at her, not sure what she's asking.

'You said people have been very mean to Ernie,' she says.

I open my mouth, then close it again.

It's a hard thing to explain, that a person can take another person's pet-grooming salon away from them out of anger and greed and unkindness and out of having a brother who's a very experienced lawyer and a new husband who's a member of the local council so they know how to do it.

Actually it's not that hard to explain.

It's just hard to say out loud that your mum is greedy and unkind.

'What sort of mean?' says the girl again.

'Just mean,' I say.

The hospital entrance is crowded, but the security guard still sees us.

'What have you got there?' he says.

'A present for a patient in Ward Six,' I say.

The security guard steps towards us, takes the parcel, and sniffs it.

'No hot food in the wards,' he says.

'It's just chips,' says the girl. 'For a family member. Take a look if you don't believe us. Taste them for identification purposes if you need to.'

I look at the girl.

The security guard looks at us both.

'Come this way,' he says sternly.

We follow him to a small room full of floor-cleaning machines. Two other security guards are sitting at a table drinking mugs of tea.

'You're not gunna believe this,' says the first security guard to the others. 'This pair want to bribe us to let them take hot chips into a ward.'

The other two security guards look at me and the girl as if we're criminals.

The first security guard plonks the parcel onto the table and rips it open. All three of them stare at the mountain of chips inside.

'Jeez,' says one. 'It'd need to be some bribe to get this lot in.'

'Help yourself,' says the girl.

I give her another look. She just can't resist giving chips away. What is this weird thing with her and potatoes?

The security guards look at each other. They reach forward and take one chip each. Then the first security guard bundles the parcel back up and puts it in my arms.

'Ward Six is on the tenth floor,' he says. 'Don't get grease on the furniture.'

In the lift, two doctors get in.

They don't need their stethoscopes to tell what's in my parcel because it's hanging open and I'm only just managing to stop chips falling onto the floor.

The doctors look at me and the girl.

'Where are you going with those?' says one.

'Ward Six,' I say.

'It's a present for a family member,' says the girl.

The doctors think about this.

'I used to live on chips when I was at med school,' says one.

'Same here,' says the other.

I know what the girl will say next. So I say it first.

'Help yourselves.'

The girl gives me a grin. I don't grin back. Uncle Mal has got a friend who's a doctor, and when he comes to dinner he always has multiple helpings of everything.

The doctors take two chips each and eat them.

They don't take more, which is a relief.

'Nice,' says one. 'Not from the canteen here, eh?'

I shake my head.

'From a real chip shop,' says the girl. 'Where they use real potatoes.'

The other doctor nods thoughtfully.

'All that erythromycin and metronidazole we pump into patients,' he says. 'Sometimes I think they'd be better off with chips.'

Ward Six must be having a quiet night because the nurses are standing around chatting.

'Hello, Jackson,' says one of the younger nurses. 'You here to see Ernie?'

I nod.

The nurse gives me and the girl a sympathetic look.

An older nurse is staring at the chips.

'You do know,' she says, 'you're not meant to bring hot food into the ward.'

'It's a present for Ernie,' says the girl.

She must be leaving the rest for me to say.

I look around at all the nurses.

'And for everyone who's caring for him,' I say.

I glance at the girl. I expect her to give me a look that says good one, we're a team. But she's wincing and frowning at me as if I've just done something wrong.

The nurses are all grinning with delight.

'That is so kind,' says one.

'I wish all our patients' families were so thoughtful,' says another.

'You two are our favourite visitors,' says the older nurse, beaming at me and the girl and taking the parcel of chips from me and putting it on the nurses' table.

The nurses all help themselves. Not just one or two chips each.

Handfuls.

They all gobble happily and some are already onto their second fistful.

I'm about to throw myself across the dwindling pile of chips to protect Ernie's present with my body.

Before I can, the girl tugs at my arm.

'Come on,' she says. 'We won't get them back now. Let's go and see Ernie.'

'No,' I want to yell. 'They're Ernie's chips. He's lost enough in his life already.'

Before I can get the words out, someone else arrives.

It's the head nurse, who can be very strict.

She stares at the chips and the munching nurses and she doesn't look happy.

Then she blinks.

Now she's staring at the girl.

'I know you,' she says. 'You're Gabby Fletcher. You poor love. A friend of mine works in the hospital that sent the ambulances for your family.'

The girl looks at the floor.

I can see she'd rather not be recognised.

A buzz is going around the nurses. A muffled buzz because they're still eating. But I can make out a few words through the mouthfuls of chips.

'She's been put in a home.'

'Tragic.'

'Both parents and her brother and sister.'

'On the Hume Highway.'

'Out-of-control potato truck.'

The girl turns to me and grabs my arm hard.

'Let's go,' she hisses.

She drags me away down the ward. I don't ask anything because some questions are too painful to think about, let alone answer.

Instead I point to Ernie's room.

We go in.

The other two patients in Ernie's room are asleep. I assume he is too at first because his eyes are closed and the machines plugged into him are beeping very slowly and quietly.

Then he opens his eyes.

He sees me and smiles. Sort of. I can see it's an effort for him to move even a few face muscles.

I go over and put my hand gently on his arm.

It's all I've got now the chips are gone.

The girl comes over too.

'Hello, Ernie,' she says softly. 'I'm Gabby. Would you like a chip?'

From her coat pocket she takes her small bag of chips and holds it out to him.

Ernie looks at the chips blankly for quite a while. Then he smiles. A proper smile this time. He takes one.

'Thank you, Gabby,' he says quietly. 'Are you a friend of Jackson's?'

Gabby looks at me.

I nod.

Gabby's eyes glow softly like the machines around the bed. She turns back to Ernie.

'Yes,' she says to him. 'I am.'

Ernie eats the chip.

It must be cold but he doesn't seem to mind.

I get a chair from the corner and put it next to Ernie's bed so Gabby can sit down. Then I go and lean against the wall, partly because there's only one chair, but mostly because it feels like the right thing to do.

I can't hear everything Ernie and Gabby are saying, but I don't mind. The more they talk, the more their faces relax and the more they smile.

I'm glad just to watch.

You don't often get to see two people without much happiness in their lives having some of it right in front of you.

I realise I'm smiling too.

It's not just the pleasure of watching Ernie and Gabby. I'm thinking about everything that's happened tonight, and I reckon Gabby was pretty smart using chips to forgive potatoes.

Because Ernie was right all along.

Chips are magic.

Secret Diary Of A Dog

M addy doesn't usually get angry, but she did today.

'Ralph,' she yelled at me.

'*Woof*,' I said, to remind Maddy that if she wags her tail, well bottom, it might help her feel a bit better.

She was shouting so loudly she didn't even hear me. Young humans make a lot of noise when they get worked up.

'Spit that out, Ralph,' Maddy yelled, 'and don't ever let me catch you using the dental floss again.'

She must have spotted some white thread hanging from my jaws. I opened my mouth and the dental floss flopped out. So did a soggy pair of Dylan's underpants.

Dylan wailed.

He's eight, so he's very fond of his Spider-Man underpants.

'That does it, Ralph,' said Maddy. 'You're grounded. No sniffing other dogs' bottoms for a week.'

Maddy obviously couldn't see that I was simply trying to help out around the house. That I was on my way to remind Dad he urgently needed to do some shopping because the dental floss had almost run out and Dylan's undies had developed serious elastic-droop.

'Bad boy,' Maddy yelled at me.

I was shocked. Maddy had never called me that before, not ever.

That's when I started to realise just how much she's feeling the stress of Mum being away.

What happened next showed it even more.

Both cats tried to slink out of the room.

'Stay right where you are, both of you,' shouted Maddy. 'Did we or did we not have an agreement?'

The cats frowned as if they were trying to remember.

'We agreed,' said Maddy, 'that if I found any more dead birds in my sock drawer you would be punished. So, no TV for a month, not even if *Animal Hospital* has a stir-fry chicken segment.'

The cats were looking confused. Not surprising, poor things. I've tried to tell them, but they still think a dead bird is the best present you can give a person.

Both the goldfish were smirking.

'As for you two,' said Maddy, 'I've had enough of your smug insolence.'

To our horror and amazement, Maddy put the goldfish over her knee and gave them a spanking.

We glanced at each other, me and Dylan and the cats, and waited for Maddy to realise that spanking isn't good, plus it wasn't really working because she had to leave the goldfish in the water and she couldn't smack the bowl too hard in case it broke.

I barked a few times, advising her of this.

'Be quiet,' yelled Maddy.

Dad came in, just as I hoped he would, and saw what Maddy was doing.

'What on earth is going on?' he said.

Dad loves all living creatures. He's a very kind man. He refuses to eat tuna if dolphins have been caught in the same net. I'm pretty sure he'd refuse to eat dolphins if tuna had in any way suffered.

'Well?' said Dad.

Maddy didn't say anything. Just stared at the goldfish guiltily.

'Alright, everyone,' said Dad. 'Calm down. I know this isn't easy, Mum being away. But we're all doing our best.'

Maddy gave him a long look.

Then she said something that helped explain why she was behaving so unlike the Maddy we know.

'Dad' she said. 'We know you're trying your best, and we love you, and we know Mum asked you not to let the house get messy, but is it really necessary for you to be the most painfully organised dad in the whole world?'

Dad frowned at her.

'What do you mean?' he said.

'The lists,' said Maddy. 'They're stressing us out. Why can't you do anything without making a list? What other parent needs a list before they do the gardening?

(1) gardening gloves

(2) gardening hat

(3) lawn mower

(4) lawn.'

Dad was still frowning.

'I'm sorry,' he said. 'I just want you to feel the house is in safe hands.'

'We want to feel that too,' said Maddy. 'Right, Dylan? Right, Ralph?'

'Yes,' said Dylan.

'*Woof,*' I replied.

'But Dad,' said Maddy. 'Can't you see? The more mega-organised you get, the more nervous we get that deep down this is all too much for you. Look at the way you put food into the fridge in alphabetical order. If Mum doesn't come home soon, I'm going to have a nervous breakdown.'

Dad didn't say anything else for quite a few moments.

Just kept on frowning, concerned and sad.

Then he perked up.

'I think we all need a day off,' he said. 'Let's go to the zoo.'

Dylan and Maddy looked stunned.

Today was a school day, and a work day for Dad.

'Come on,' said Dad. 'Car leaves in ten minutes. Ralph can come too if he stays in the backpack.'

Maddy opened her mouth as if she had more to say.

Then she changed her mind, and she and Dylan ran off to get ready.

Dad picked me up and tickled my tummy. But he wasn't grinning like he usually does when he tickles me.

'Wish me luck, Ralph,' he muttered.

He put me back down and went off to get ready himself.

I watched him go. I had a heavy lump in my tummy. It wasn't a fur ball, or one of those white balls you eat when you go to a golf course.

It was a ball of anxiety.

I took my own advice and wagged my tail to calm myself down.

Chill, I said. There's nothing to worry about. We're just going to the zoo for a fun day out.

Woof.

I love the zoo.

When you live in a house with humans, you don't get to meet many other creatures from the wild. Meeting noble creatures from the wild makes my heart soar with pride. It makes me feel a bit noble and wild myself, even if I am wearing a crocheted tartan doggy smock.

Trouble is, dogs aren't allowed to run around at the zoo. They're not even meant to be there. Which is why I had to stay in Dylan's backpack.

Oh well, at least it gave me time to do my diary.

People think dogs don't keep diaries, but we do. In our heads. It's quite hard work. That's why we spend a lot of time panting. Having your tongue out cools your brain down.

I wish humans knew how to do that. Maddy could have done it today during the dental-floss incident. And at the zoo when Dad sat her and Dylan down for a little chat.

'You're probably wondering,' he said to them, 'why I've brought you here.'

'Dad,' said Maddy. 'This is the zoo. There's only one reason people come to the zoo.'

'To look at animals,' said Dylan. 'And have ice-cream.'

I peeked out from the backpack, hoping Dad would say, spot on, that's it, absolutely right.

But he didn't.

He seemed to be having trouble getting the next lot of words out.

'Except,' said Maddy to Dad, 'last time we were here, we did spend quite a lot of time trying to get your camera back from that orangutan.'

The kids both chuckled at the memory.

Dad wasn't chuckling. I could see he had something serious to say and wasn't sure how to say it.

I growled a couple of times, softly, to encourage him to spit it out, whatever it was. The birds and animals chattering and screeching and grunting around us all agreed.

'Tell them,' snorted the zebras.

'You can't pull wool over kids' eyes,' screeched the toucans.

'Only a fool would try,' grunted the hippos. Though that might have been, 'Only a fool would try to get an orangutan to take a photo of him and his family.'

Both Maddy and Dylan were looking at Dad, concerned.

'Are you alright?' said Maddy.

'Would you like a lick of my ice-cream?' said Dylan. 'When you've bought it?'

'Mum rang late last night,' said Dad. 'I'm afraid she's going to be away longer than we thought.'

Maddy and Dylan stared at him.

'Longer?' said Dylan.

'How much longer?' said Maddy.

They both looked so shocked, I wanted to hug them. But dogs can't hug. We can only lick. And it's a bit hard when you're in a backpack.

I did my best with Dylan's ear.

'Grandad's not getting better as quickly as we'd hoped,' said Dad quietly. 'Mum will tell you about it tonight when we Skype, but she could be away a few more months.'

Maddy and Dylan were looking at Dad in horror.

My stomach was knotted. Over my left shoulder I could hear a pale-throated sloth regurgitating its lunch. I knew how it felt.

'A few months?' said Maddy.

Dad nodded.

Everything went very quiet. Even the sloth.

'I want to go to Scotland,' said Maddy. 'I want to be with Mum and Grandad.'

'Me too,' said Dylan.

I didn't woof 'me too' because I knew what Dad's reply would be. Plus when dogs fly they have to spend weeks in a cage with only suitcases to talk to.

Dad sighed.

'I'm sorry, loves,' he said. 'We can't afford it.'

Maddy glared at him.

I knew what she was thinking.

Sell the car. Sell the house. Sell Dylan's Lego.

But she didn't say any of that because she knew it was impossible. There was school to go to and work to do and me to feed.

Dad struggled to put on a cheerful face.

'It's not the end of the world,' he said. 'We'll still Skype with Mum every day. And maybe it'll only be one or two months.'

Poor Dad.

I knew that despite his brave face his heart must be heavier than a buffalo's bum flap.

Maddy and Dylan looked like theirs definitely were.

'Sometimes,' said Dad, still struggling to sound

positive, 'every family has to be apart for a while. Like those kids at your school who live with their father.'

'Their mum's dead,' said Maddy.

'Oh,' said Dad.

'And it's easier for them,' said Dylan. 'Their dad's got an apartment with a swimming pool and a housekeeper and a speedboat.'

'Oh,' said Dad.

I've never heard him sound so miserable.

Poor humans. They're always worried that other humans are better than them. Dogs don't have that problem. It's because we're allowed to sniff each other's bottoms.

'I know how hard this is for you,' said Dad to Maddy and Dylan. 'I wanted to soften the blow a bit. That's why I brought you here today. To your favourite place.'

'Too see the animals,' said Maddy. 'And take our minds off the fact that we're living with a parent who uses a tape measure to make toast fingers.'

Dad looked hurt. But he knew it was true.

'I'll get some ice-creams,' he mumbled and hurried away towards the kiosk.

Maddy took me out of the backpack and buried her face in my fur.

'Oh, Ralph,' she sobbed. 'I don't want months without Mum. I miss her. It wouldn't be so bad if Dad would just relax and be a normal dad, instead of trying to be so ridiculously organised and tidy.'

'I don't want him to buy me new undies,' wailed Dylan. 'He'll buy organised ones.'

'We can't even tell Mum,' said Maddy. 'She'll worry.'

I was tempted to offer to bite Dad's bottom, not hard, just enough to snap him out of it. But I knew Maddy and Dylan wouldn't be comfortable with that, and Dad definitely wouldn't.

'Dad used to be so relaxed and confident,' said Maddy. 'Before Mum went. I want that Dad back.'

'Me too,' said Dylan. 'I'm scared to eat the toast fingers.'

I had an idea. Perhaps I could just gently pull a few of Dad's leg hairs out with my teeth.

Then I had a better idea.

Of course.

I wriggled out of Maddy's arms, jumped to the ground and without looking back I ran.

It was risky. I'd heard rumours that if zoo keepers catch dogs running around the zoo, they feed them to the pythons. But it was worth the risk.

I reached the lion enclosure and stuck my head between the bars.

'Excuse me,' I woofed to a magnificent male lion from the wild who was stretched out in the sun. 'Could you do me a favour? In a few moments a couple of human kids will arrive. Could you demonstrate how in the natural world daddies are very good at looking after children? Just be big and strong and kind and gentle, but very fierce when it comes to protecting cubs.'

The lion gave me an unfriendly stare. He didn't look like a creature who did many favours. Not kind and gentle ones.

I peered around, trying to see his family.

'Where are the cubs?' I asked the lion.

At the back of the enclosure was a cave. Perhaps they were inside, watching TV or chewing on a wildebeest.

A female lion came out of the cave.

'The kids are in a separate enclosure,' she growled. 'So Daddy Big-Chops here won't eat them.'

I stared at her, horrified. What sort of psychopath was she married to?

The female lion rolled her eyes.

'Don't ask,' she growled. 'They all do it. Quirk of nature, they reckon. They don't mention it when they first ask you out, of course.'

I heard yells and saw Maddy and Dylan sprinting towards me.

'Sorry to bother you,' I said to the lions, and dashed over to the elephant compound.

'Quick,' I barked at a herd of elephants. 'All you dads. Look loving and capable. I want these kids to see you and think, behold the mighty elephant, reliable and patient and never forgets a birthday.'

Several female elephants gave me a look.

'They may never forget a birthday,' said one, 'but they usually forget their kids. Last year one of the big boofheads rolled over and squashed a few to death.'

I gave the mummy elephant a cross look.

Honesty is good, but there's a time and a place.

'If you want to see the champion dad of the natural world,' said another female elephant, 'try the insect pavilion. There's a beetle in there that eats its own poo so his kids won't catch germs from it.'

That sounded promising, but I wanted Maddy and Dylan to see that big creatures, human-size ones, could be good daddies too.

Maddy and Dylan were very close.

I veered over to the hippo pit.

'Guys,' I said. 'Please. Work with me. Be good dads.'

Maddy and Dylan arrived, panting and angry.

'Ralph,' yelled Maddy. 'What are you thinking? You know you don't run off like that. Bad boy.'

I winced, then pointed my nose towards the hippos.

We all looked at a large male hippo lying in a pool of mud. Unfortunately he didn't look like a great parent. He wasn't cuddling his kids, or giving them tips on personal hygiene, or listening to their problems, or training them in their chosen sport, or helping them with their homework. Forget being relaxed and spontaneous with toast fingers, he didn't look like he knew what a toast finger was.

'His kids are over there,' said Dylan. 'He growls at them if they try to get close.'

This wasn't what I'd hoped for.

The only individuals the daddy hippo would allow near him were some white birds with long beaks who were clambering all over him, eating things off his tummy.

'He's organised them,' said Maddy, disgusted. 'To groom him. Pick fleas off him while he has a snooze. Trim his dry skin. Make him all neat. That'll be us soon, forced to collect our dad's dandruff and count it.'

Dylan gave a groan of despair.

I felt like groaning myself.

I could see Dad heading towards us, ice-creams safely cradled in his hands. Nobody organises ice-creams better than Dad.

Sometimes, when you're desperate, you don't think, you just act.

Well, we dogs do.

I squeezed between the bars of the enclosure and flung myself down into the hippo pit.

The mud was deeper than it looked. And stickier. And smellier. And the hippos' teeth were yellower than they looked, and more crooked, and much sharper.

Even the young hippos' teeth were.

The young hippos were grunting and squealing with indignation. So were the birds. They glared at me and I knew how the daddy hippo's fleas must feel.

Except the fleas weren't having to struggle to keep their heads above the mud like me.

'Cool,' said the daddy hippo. 'We normally don't get fed till four o'clock. Hey, you're a seriously plump swamp rat. Nice tartan packaging too.'

Other daddy hippos lumbered towards me, and a few mummies. All licking their lips.

I started to think I should have given this plan a bit more thought.

Then I heard my name being yelled, louder then it had all day. Not angrily, like before. Heroically.

And not by Maddy.

By Dad.

Suddenly he was in the mud next to me, just as I'd hoped, thrashing around, driving the hippos back with big sweeps of his arm and sprays of mud and dollops of ice-cream.

'Whoa,' said the first hippo. 'Take it easy, dude. We're a protected species. Is that vanilla?'

The next few moments were a blur. Dad dragged me out of the mud, and while he heaved us both over the railings, I spent a bit of time upside down in his armpit, which was much nicer than the hippo pit.

Then Maddy and Dylan were hugging me and neither of them seemed to mind how muddy they got or how many other zoo visitors took photos of their muddiness.

'Ralph,' said Maddy, 'why did you do that?'

I didn't try to tell them. Sometimes it's better to keep quiet, specially when your mouth's full of hippos' lounge room.

Then Maddy and Dylan hugged Dad for ages, which made them even muddier.

'You saved Ralph's life, Dad,' said Dylan.

'And you risked yours,' said Maddy.

After the hugging, Dad went back to checking me over for injuries. There weren't any, luckily. But Dad didn't stop till he'd made absolutely sure.

He didn't seem to care that mud and slime and hippo poo were oozing out of my doggie smock, even though he'd crocheted it himself.

While he checked me over, I saw the way Maddy and Dylan were looking at him. At his sticky hair and his ripped shirt and his one shoe missing and at the mud and slime and hippo poo oozing out of his pockets.

I could see in their eyes they'd realised something.

Something that, if only I could speak, I could have told them a long time ago.

That their dad is a brave and noble creature from the wild, and no matter how long Mum is away, they'll be OK.

'Dad,' said Maddy. 'After you've persuaded the zoo officials not to call the police, can we go home and have toast fingers?'

'And after that,' said Dylan, 'can you buy me some new underpants?'

Snot Chocolate

It's been a long trial. Nearly two weeks so far. Mum must be exhausted. I think that's why she's doing the amazing thing she's doing now.

'Ms Beckwell,' growls the judge. 'Are you eating?'

Everyone in the courtroom stares at Mum. A couple of people snigger. The prosecutor rolls his eyes. The jury looks jealous.

Mum swallows whatever she's got in her mouth.

I'm shocked. When Mum started letting me come here after school to watch her work, the first thing she said was never eat in a courtroom.

The judge is glaring at Mum.

Mum hesitates. I'm pretty sure she'll own up. The truth is important to her. She spends a lot of time advising her clients to tell it.

'Sorry, your Honour,' says Mum.

The judge growls.

The jury looks wistful.

The prosecutor, whose tummy looks like he does a lot of eating himself, goes back to questioning one of the defendants about the alleged crime.

I'm sitting up the back in my favourite seat, the one that lets me see everything Mum does. I can see what she's doing now. Fiddling with something under her table.

It's a chocolate wrapper.

Now I'm really shocked.

Mum's eating chocolate in court. Which is a bad thing to do in any courtroom, but a really bad thing to do in a courtroom where the two defendants' alleged crime is stealing three hundred and twenty-eight thousand dollars worth of Easter animals.

Chocolate ones.

'I put it to you,' the prosecutor says to one of the defendants, 'that the nine hundred and three boxes of chocolate bilbies found in your storage unit came from the same hijacked truck as the five thousand two hundred and seventeen boxes of chocolate bunnies also found in your storage unit, or should I say, in your storehouse of crime.'

'It's not a storehouse of crime,' says the defendant. 'No way.'

I look across at Mum to see if she's going to object to what the prosecutor said. She's a brilliant defence lawyer and she doesn't let prosecutors get away with anything. But this time she stays silent. Mostly because her mouth is full.

I can't believe it.

If I was a defendant, I'd be very cross that my barrister couldn't speak up because she had a gobful of Dairy Milk.

The defendants don't seem to have noticed.

Neither, luckily, has the judge.

The jury has. All twelve of them are staring at Mum. A few are licking their lips. It's ages since lunch and I don't think the criminal justice system includes afternoon tea.

Then the chocolate penny drops.

I realise what Mum is doing.

She's reminding the members of the jury how irresistible chocolate is. So that if they find Theodore Conway Tucker and Christopher Waylon Tucker guilty of stealing a truckload of it, they'll be a bit understanding and recommend a light sentence. Weekend detention picking up chocolate wrappers in a supermarket carpark, something like that.

Phew, I was worried there for a moment.

I thought Mum was being a greedy pig, but she's just being a good lawyer.

'Mum,' I groan. 'What are you doing?'

I stagger into her bedroom. It's the middle of the night. I was fast asleep until the noise from her bedroom woke me up.

'Sorry, love,' says Mum. 'Have I got it up too loud?'

She's in bed with her iPad. Sometimes she can't sleep so she watches movies. But it's not the iPad

143

I'm staring at. It's the chocolate wrappers all over her bed.

'What are you doing?' I say.

'I was a bit peckish,' says Mum.

'Peckish?' I say, still staring at the remains of half a chocolate shop on her duvet. 'That's not peckish, that's being a greedy pig.'

Mum loses it.

'Jemma,' she says angrily. 'How dare you speak to me like that. Go back to bed.'

But I don't. I stand there, glaring at her. Just like I've seen her do to a cop in court who won't give her a straight answer.

Finally Mum sighs.

'I felt like a bit of chocolate,' she says. 'Is that a crime?'

'A bit of chocolate?' I feel like saying. 'A bit?'

But I don't because this isn't a courtroom and it's not a good idea to cross-examine your own parent when she's already furious.

'You don't even like chocolate,' I say quietly.

'I just got out of the habit of eating it,' says Mum. 'I used to love it when I was a kid. And last week, when I had to sit through all those hours of expert witnesses testifying how the bunnies and bilbies in the defendants' warehouse had exactly the same smooth and creamy cocoa butter content as the stolen chocolate, I started tasting it again. My imagination started salivating. My taste buds went crazy. So I got myself a bar.'

I don't know what to say.

That actually sounds quite reasonable.

'But when you eat it in court,' I say, 'that's for the jury, right? So they're reminded how easily people are tempted by chocolate, specially eleven and a half tonnes of it.'

Mum looks at me, frowning.

'That is the reason you've been eating it in court,' I say. 'To get your clients a lighter sentence?'

Mum grins.

'That is so clever,' she says. 'I didn't think of that. You're going to make a great lawyer one day.'

It isn't the reason.

There's another reason Mum's eating chocolate in court, and it's making me sick in the stomach just thinking about it.

We're in court now and the jury's been sent out because they're not allowed to hear a legal argument that has to happen between Mum and the prosecutor.

Mum has explained to me that these legal arguments are a very important part of a trial. And she's very good at them. But today her words aren't flowing like they usually do. Mostly because she popped three squares of Lindt Extra Creamy into her mouth just before she started speaking.

'Are you alright, Ms Beckwell?' says the judge. 'Do you need a glass of water?'

'I'm fine, thank you, your Honour,' says Mum, swallowing.

She's not fine.

I've just realised the horrible truth. My own mother is addicted to chocolate. Which is putting her career seriously at risk. Not to mention her health. We did it at school. Sugar is poison. Too much gives you diabetes, tooth decay and chocolate stains on your sheets.

Well I'm not sitting here and letting it happen.

Mum might not be able to save Theodore Conway Tucker and Christopher Waylon Tucker, but I'm going to save her.

Mum's gone to bed.

I thought she never would.

When Mum decides we need a family talk, it can go on for hours.

At least this evening she confessed. Admitted she's been overdoing the chocolate lately. Though it wasn't so much a confession as an excuse. She reckons she needs cheering up because things have been a bit bleak since Dad left.

I could have told her that.

'Mum,' I said. 'If work's not bringing enough joy into your life, find yourself a hobby or a project. Weeding national parks or volunteer dog walking or something.'

I didn't tell her what my new project is.

Getting her off chocolate.

Good, it's melted.

I give the rich smooth liquid a stir, careful not

to rattle the saucepan on the cooktop. Mum's bedroom is right up at the other end of the house from the kitchen, but sounds travel more at night and a chocolate addict can probably hear chocolate from streets away.

Now for the magic ingredient.

I sprinkle a big spoonful of dried chilli powder into the melted chocolate and give it another stir.

We learned about this at school too. If you have a very painful experience, it can turn you off nice things you were doing at the time. Like if you're wearing green shoes and a dog pees on your feet, it can put you off wearing green shoes ever again. Specially if the yellow pee turns the green shoes blue, which is my least favourite colour.

It's called psychology.

I pour the molten chocolate and chilli into the ice-cube mould and put it into the fridge.

It'll be set by morning. I'll get up very early and put the squares back into the gourmet-chocolate-shop bag. When I give it to Mum as a sorry-for-calling-you-a-greedy-pig present, it'll look like ordinary chocolate.

The man in the gourmet chocolate shop said this type of chocolate is perfect for melting and re-setting.

'Are you going to make shapes?' he asked. 'Easter bunnies?'

I shook my head.

The only shape I'm interested in making is

Mum's mouth screwed up into a I'm-never-eating-chocolate-again shape.

I still can't believe it.

'Thank you, sweetheart,' said Mum on our way home from court yesterday. 'Your present was delicious. How did you know I love chilli chocolate?'

I stared at her, but she didn't notice.

Just gave me a kiss.

Her breath smelled of chocolate. And chilli.

I waited till we'd had dinner and watched TV and she was in bed, and then I crept into the kitchen again. I peered into the fridge.

To save Mum I needed something that would make chocolate taste truly revolting.

I saw the perfect thing.

Fish.

A piece of leftover raw snapper from the fish cakes Mum and I made for dinner.

I chopped it into tiny pieces, melted some chocolate and stirred the fish in. I added a slurp of Asian fish sauce just to make sure.

What a waste of time.

When I got to court this afternoon, Mum wasn't looking even a tiny bit like she wanted to vomit.

She was busy questioning the driver of the chocolate truck. Gently, because he looked upset. He'd lost his job and said that since the trauma of being robbed he'd also completely lost his appetite for chocolate.

Mum didn't comment on that, but I could see she felt very sorry for him.

'Did you see the faces of the individuals who robbed you?' she asked him.

'No,' he said. 'They had Donald Duck masks on.'

'Would you recognise them from their clothes or the shape of their bodies?' asked Mum.

In the dock, Theodore Conway Tucker and Christopher Waylon Tucker both tried to make themselves look very small.

'No,' said the driver. 'They were wearing bumble bee onesies.'

Mum said 'no more questions' and sat down and while the judge was telling the truck driver he could go, she popped a piece of fish chocolate into her mouth.

And sucked it happily.

I had to control myself. You're not allowed to scream with frustration in the public seats of a courtroom.

I wondered if Theodore Conway Tucker and Christopher Waylon Tucker would be interested in robbing Mum of all her chocolate.

Probably not.

On the way home I didn't want to talk.

Mum did.

'That chocolate you gave me this morning,' she said. 'It was very different to the last lot. A very complex and delicious flavour. What was it?'

'Gourmet,' I muttered.

'You certainly know how to come up with yummy chocolate,' said Mum. 'But love, please, maybe not quite so much. I don't want to get fat.'

I was tempted to remind her about something else she doesn't want to get.

Fired.

If the judge had seen Mum stuffing her face with fish chocolate, her career would be in worse shape than Exhibit A27 on the evidence table, which is a yellow and black striped ski glove that got dropped at the scene of the crime and squashed by a bus.

I didn't say that to Mum.

Mothers who are lawyers just love arguments, and Mum's problem is too serious to waste time squabbling.

It's so serious, I'm doing something I never thought I'd do.

Creeping into Mum's room at two a.m.

Checking she's asleep, which she is, I can tell by the snoring.

Hoping she's had a sleeping pill, which she often does, specially since Dad hasn't been around.

Keeping my torch pointing to the carpet as I reach out and very carefully insert a cotton bud into Mum's nostril.

And gently turn it.

If this doesn't get Mum off chocolate, nothing will.

* * *

150

It's slow work, gathering somebody else's snot in secret. You don't get a lot for your efforts. Specially not the solid bits you need to make snot chocolate. Solid bits are extremely important if you want the person who eats the snot chocolate to really taste the snot.

After three nights I still don't have enough.

I've agonised about this, but I'll have to do it.

Add some of my own.

I can't risk waiting any longer. The harder Mum works to prove that Theodore Conway Tucker and Christopher Waylon Tucker didn't steal all that chocolate, the more chocolate she eats.

Today she ate heaps, just after Theodore and Christopher told the prosecutor they'd lost the address of the caravan park in East Gippsland where they say they bought the chocolate.

She ate some more when the prosecutor asked them about the colour of the caravan they say the seller had the chocolate stored in.

'I can't remember,' said Theodore. 'It was just an ordinary colour.'

'Brown?' said the prosecutor with a sneer.

Mum put four squares of chocolate into her mouth at that point, I saw her. I think the judge might have seen her as well.

I need snot chocolate and I need it fast.

So here we go, in goes some of mine, straight from the nostril into the saucepan.

I'm her daughter, after all.

It would only be a health risk if it was from a stranger. One living in a caravan park in East Gippsland, for example.

This is weird.

It's the first day of the school holidays and I've been here in court all day and Mum hasn't eaten a single piece of chocolate the whole time. I can see the bag from the chocolate shop sticking out of her briefcase under the table, and it hasn't even been opened.

Mum seems pretty stressed.

Maybe that's why she hasn't eaten any chocolate.

She has to do her closing speech to the jury soon, and things aren't looking good for Theodore Conway Tucker and Christopher Waylon Tucker.

Theodore and Christopher aren't looking good either.

Every day of this trial, they've looked more and more guilty. Sitting slumped in a guilty way. Staring at the floor in a guilty way. And if anyone mentions a bunny or a bilby or a baby chocolate animal of any type, the defendants look like they're going to burst into tears.

Mum's about to stand up, I can tell by the way her shoulders are going tense.

Hang on, they're relaxing again. She's reaching under the table. Opening the chocolate bag. Popping a piece of chocolate into her mouth.

A piece of snot chocolate.

She's sucking it. Chewing it.

Thinking about it with a frown.

I wish she wasn't eating it right now. The judge is instructing her to present her closing remarks to the jury. But I can see she's more concerned with what's in her mouth.

As you would be if you were having your first taste of snot chocolate.

Mum stands up. Starts speaking to the jury. Stops. Moves her tongue around her teeth. Frowns again, as if there's something she can't work out.

'Ms Beckwell,' growls the judge, louder than he's growled this whole trial. 'Are you eating again?'

Mum looks at him, startled. She doesn't reply.

'I'm a patient man,' says the judge, angrily and even more loudly. 'But your behaviour throughout this trial has been, I don't know how else to describe it, a trial. You're very lucky I don't dismiss you from these proceedings. One more transgression and I will refer you to the disciplinary board.'

Poor Mum has gone pale.

It's like she's suddenly realised what she's been doing these last few days. Risking her career. Risking her clients' defence.

Or maybe she's just suddenly realised what she's eating.

'Thank you, Jemma,' says Mum suddenly across the dinner table.

She's been very quiet since we got home, and I

haven't said anything because I wanted to give her enough time to digest the judge's warning today, and the snot.

I'm not sure what she's thanking me for. Peeling the veggies? Offering to stack the dishwasher?

'I know what you've been doing, love,' says Mum quietly.

My blood runs colder than chocolate ice-cream.

Mum doesn't look angry, but her eyes have got that look in them. The lawyer's look that says nobody will leave this room until the truth is admitted.

'If you wanted to put me off chocolate,' says Mum, 'you should have used coriander. It's about the only thing I hate the taste of.'

I could kick myself.

How could I have forgotten about a simple herb? And Mum reckons I'll make a great lawyer.

Forget that.

Forget everything, except what's going to happen now.

Mum knows what I did.

Will she get ill and depressed again, like she did with Dad when he did bad things?

'That was rough luck,' says Mum, 'forgetting how much I love chilli. And fish, specially used in creative ways. But what was that last flavour? It was salty and bitter and sweet at the same time. Some kind of salted caramel?'

I don't say anything.

She looks at me, hard.

I've seen politicians in court flinch when she does that. Tough politicians. Politicians who don't even flinch when they tell lies about drowned refugee children.

I can't help it, I have to tell her the truth.

'Snot,' I say.

Mum keeps looking at me for a long time.

Then she smiles.

'I love you,' she says.

We're waiting for the jury to come back in and give their decision.

Mum's not eating chocolate today, or doodling on a legal notepad like the prosecutor.

She looks calm.

Sad but calm.

I know now why she's sad. She explained last night. Theodore Conway Tucker and Christopher Waylon Tucker stole the chocolate bunnies and bilbies for a reason. Their sister's baby was very sick and needed an operation that could only be done in America and would cost two hundred and eighty thousand dollars. Theodore and Christopher were going to sell the chocolate to raise the money. But before they could, the baby died.

I glance over at Theodore and Christopher.

No wonder they're sitting slumped and staring at the floor.

I look around, trying to see their sister.

Her name's Eileen and she's been in the public

seats every day of the trial. She always looks sad too. I thought it was just because she was worried about her brothers.

Eileen isn't here today.

She probably can't bear the thought of seeing Theodore and Christopher being found guilty and sent to jail.

The judge comes back into the courtroom.

This means the jury are on their way back to give their verdict.

The judge sits in his big seat.

Mum sits back down and stares at her table. I know what she's doing. Trying to stay composed. She explained last night that this is the saddest trial she's ever worked on. Every time she looks at Theodore and Christopher and Eileen, she wants to burst into tears. The only way she's stopped herself is by eating chocolate. It's something she used to do as a kid when she was very sad.

She's not eating chocolate now.

She's staying composed without it.

I think she's doing the mental exercise I told her about last night. The one where you forget where you are and travel in your mind to a happy place.

When I do it I go to Cairns where Mum and Dad and I had a holiday when I was little.

I don't think Mum's in Cairns. Her shoulders aren't in the right position for whitewater rafting. She's probably planning what she's going to say after Theodore and Christopher are found guilty.

She couldn't say in the trial why they did it, because she was trying to convince the jury that they didn't do it. Now she's hoping that when she explains, the judge will give them a light sentence.

Her elbows are on the table and her cheeks are cupped in her hands.

Except what's happening?

One of her hands is moving round to the front of her face. Her finger is going up her nose. And out again. And into her mouth.

Oh no.

She's still gazing at the table.

She's chewing, but I can see from her glazed expression she doesn't know what she's chewing.

The judge does. He's staring at her. But he doesn't say anything. I don't think he can believe what he just saw. A top lawyer picking her nose and eating it.

If she does it again though, he will believe it.

She does it again.

Oh no.

What have I done?

I gave my mother snot chocolate, and now she's developed a taste for snot.

I couldn't stay in the courtroom.

I needed quiet time to think, and there wasn't any quiet time after the jury came back in and said 'not guilty'.

People clapped and cheered. They must have

been friends of Theodore and Christopher. The court officials yelled at them to be silent.

It was chaos.

Theodore and Christopher looked as stunned as Mum.

But now I've had a chance to think, I reckon I know what happened.

The jury must have felt sorry for Mum because of the way the judge yelled at her after she ate the snot chocolate. They must have thought it was unjust. So when they found they had some doubts about the case, to do with the Donald Duck masks and the bumble bee onesies and the black and yellow striped ski glove, they must have decided to give Mum and her clients the benefit of those doubts to make up for the injustice.

Which is a great result for Theodore and Christopher.

But not so great for Mum. When word gets around that she eats her own snot, she'll probably never work again.

The thought of that makes me do what Theodore and Christopher did. Not steal eleven and a half tonnes of chocolate. Slump and stare at the floor.

I pull myself together and sit up straight. I got Mum into this, I've got to get her out of it.

I look around, desperate for ideas.

And see somebody else, over on the other side of the courthouse foyer, also slumped and staring at the floor.

And crying.

It's Eileen. Theodore and Christopher's sister.

I've never spoken to her. I don't know what to say to her now. But she looks so miserable, I can't just ignore her.

I go over.

She looks up at me.

'You're Despina Beckwell's daughter, right?' she says, wiping her eyes.

I nod.

'Tell your mum thank you from me,' says Eileen. 'She did a good job. Shame she couldn't tell the jury why the boys did it. Might have stopped them going to jail.'

She starts crying again.

'They're not going to jail,' I say.

Eileen looks at me.

I tell her about the not guilty verdict.

Eileen stares at me as if I'm a kid making things up. Then she remembers I'm not just any kid, I'm the daughter of a senior barrister.

Her face lights up.

Then falls again.

I can see what she's thinking. Her brothers were found not guilty, but she just told me they did it.

'It's OK,' I say quietly. 'I don't talk about my mum's work. Plus you can't be found guilty of something once you've been found not guilty.'

Eileen's face shows that she's having a lot of different feelings. Relief, but a lot of others as well.

I can't imagine what she must be going through. Well, sort of, but not really.

'It's a mess,' says Eileen. 'All that stolen chocolate. Our mum's gunna kill Theo and Chris. They'll wish they were in jail by the time she's finished with them.'

I try to think how I can help.

Theodore and Christopher don't deserve to be killed. Perhaps there's something I can do to help their mum calm down. Perhaps by putting all that chocolate to good use.

You can probably guess the first idea I had.

Take all the chocolate to our place so Mum can eat it every time she's tempted to pick her nose.

I thought seriously about doing that, but then I had a better idea.

One that might help Eileen, just a bit.

Here at the Children's Hospital they can't believe it. The nurses and kids are agog.

Eleven and a half tonnes of chocolate.

The nurses are letting us give an armful to each kid. And a bedful to the ones who can't sit up. They can't eat it all now of course, but the doctors have said they'll prescribe some each day to everyone who's allowed. And give lots to their families. Enough to cheer everyone up.

Theodore and Christopher are looking very cheered up.

And their mum seems to like the idea too. She

hasn't tried to kill Theodore or Christopher once.

Eileen hasn't said anything, but she's been giving lots of the children hugs and just now she gave me one.

So I think it might have helped a bit.

I keep glancing nervously at Mum. She's standing with a couple of the doctors, watching us, smiling.

She hasn't picked her nose yet.

I take a chocolate bunny over to her.

'In case you're feeling a bit emotional,' I say. 'And need something to eat.'

She takes it, but doesn't eat it.

'I want to feel emotional,' she says quietly. 'Seeing all this. Knowing it was your idea.'

I see her eyes are wet. But she looks so proud at the same time that I feel myself glowing. In an anxious sort of way.

Mum looks at me for a moment and sees what I'm thinking. She puts her finger up her nose. Just briefly. Then smiles.

'The nose-picking was for the jury,' she says. 'I wanted to show them I wasn't scared of the judge. So that when they thought about their verdict, they'd know they didn't have to be scared of him either.'

I'm so proud of my mum. She is a great lawyer.

Plus I feel very relieved.

'If you want something to worry about,' says Mum, 'my next case is defending somebody who's been accused of forging a rare and expensive painting. So chances are I'll develop a craving for oil paint and turps.'

She gives me a wink.

I grin back.

'When you've finished your work here,' says Mum, 'I'm going to take you to a very posh restaurant to show how proud I am of you. We'll order anything you want. Fillet steak, lobster, giant pizza, anything.'

'Thanks,' I say.

I have a thought.

'And when we get there,' I say, 'we can toast the great job you did in court.'

'You're a bit young for wine,' says Mum.

I give her another grin.

'I know,' I say. 'So let's both have hot chocolate.'

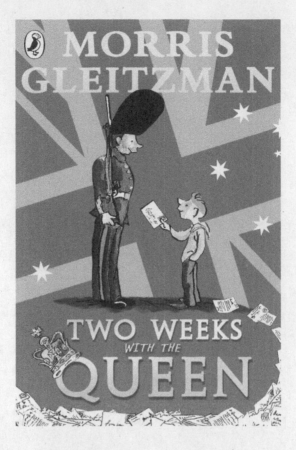

Two Weeks With The Queen

'I need to see the Queen about my sick brother.'

Colin Mudford is on a quest. His brother is very ill and
the doctors in Australia don't seem to be able to cure
him. Colin reckons it's up to him to find the best doctor
in the world. And how better to do this than by asking
the Queen for help?

Bumface

His mum calls him Mr Dependable,
but Angus can barely cope. Another baby would
be a disaster. So Angus comes up with a bold and
brave plan to stop her getting pregnant.
That's when he meets Rindi.
And Angus thought *he* had problems . . .

A moving and page-turning book' – *Sunday Times*

Boy Overboard

Jamal and Bibi have a dream. To lead Australia
to soccer glory in the next World Cup.
But first they must face landmines,
pirates, storms and assassins.
Can Jamal and his family survive their
incredible journey and get to Australia?

MORRIS GLEITZMAN

Everybody
deserves
to have
something good in their life.

At least
Once.

Once

Once I escaped from an orphanage
to find Mum and Dad.
Once I saved a girl called Zelda from a burning house.
Once I made a Nazi with a toothache laugh.
My name is Felix.
This is my story.